D1135552

CAPTIVE IN THE SPOTLIGHT

CAPTIVE IN THE SPOTLIGHT

BY

ANNIE WEST

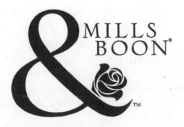

In memory of our special Daisy,
canine member of the family for
almost sixteen years and ever-supportive
writer's companion.

And with heartfelt thanks to
Josie, Serena and Antony for your advice
on Italian language, law and locations.

CHAPTER ONE

FOR FIVE GRIM years Lucy had imagined her first day of freedom. A sky the pure blue of Italian summer. The scent of citrus in the warm air and the sound of birds.

Instead she inhaled a familiar aroma. Bricks, concrete and cold steel should have no scent. Yet mixed with despair and commercial strength detergent, they created a perfume called 'Institution'. It had filled her nostrils for years.

Lucy repressed a shudder of fear, her stomach cramping.

What if there had been a mistake? What if the huge metal door before her remained firmly shut?

Panic welled at the thought of returning to her cell. To come so close then have freedom denied would finally destroy her.

The guard punched in the release code. Lucy moved close, her bag in one clammy hand, her heart in her mouth. Finally the door opened and she stepped through.

Exhaust fumes instead of citrus. Lowering grey skies instead of blue. The roar of cars rather than birdsong.

She didn't care. *She was free!*

She closed her eyes, savouring this moment she'd dreamed of since the terror engulfed her.

She was free to do as she chose. Free to try taking up the threads of her life. She'd take a cheap flight to London and a night to regroup before finishing the trip to Devon. A night somewhere quiet, with a comfortable bed and unlimited hot water.

The door clanged shut and her eyes snapped open.

A noise made her turn. Further along, by the main entrance, a crowd stirred. A crowd with cameras and microphones that blared 'Press'.

Ice scudded down Lucy's spine as she stepped briskly in the opposite direction.

She'd barely begun walking when the hubbub erupted: running feet, shouts, the roar of a motorbike.

'Lucy! Lucy Knight!' Even through the blood pounding in her ears and the confusion of so many people yelling at once, there was no mistaking the hunger in those voices. It was as if the horde had been starved and the scent of fresh blood sent them into a frenzy.

Lucy quickened her pace but a motorbike cut off

her escape. The passenger snapped off shot after shot of her stunned face before she could gather herself.

By that time the leaders of the pack had surrounded her, clamouring close and thrusting microphones in her face. It was all she could do not to give in to panic and run. After the isolation she'd known the eager crush was terrifying.

'How does it feel, Lucy?'

'What are your plans?'

'Have you anything to say to our viewers, Lucy? Or to the Volpe family?'

The bedlam of shouted questions eased a fraction at mention of the Volpe family. Lucy sucked in a shocked breath as cameras clicked and whirred in her face, disorienting her.

She should have expected this. Why hadn't she?

Because it was five years ago. Old news.

Because she'd expected the furore to die down.

What more did they want? They'd already taken so much.

If only she'd accepted the embassy's offer to spirit her to the airport. Foolishly she'd been determined to rely on no one. Five years ago British officials hadn't been able to save her from the grinding wheels of Italian justice. She'd stopped expecting help from there, or anywhere.

Look where her pride had got her!

Lips set in a firm line, she strode forward, cleaving a path through the persistent throng. She didn't shove or threaten, just kept moving with a strength and determination she'd acquired the hard way.

She was no longer the innocent eighteen-year-old who'd been incarcerated. She'd given up waiting for justice, much less a champion.

She'd had to be her own champion.

Lucy made no apology when her stride took her between a news camera and journalist wearing too much make-up and barely any skirt. The woman's attempt to coax a comment ended when her microphone fell beneath Lucy's feet.

Lucy looked neither right nor left, knowing if she stopped she'd be lost. The swelling noise and press of so many bodies sent her hurtling towards claustrophobic panic. She shook inside, her breathing grew choppy, her stomach diving as she fought the urge to flee.

The press would love that!

There was a gap ahead. Lucy made for it, to discover herself surrounded by big men in dark suits and sunglasses. Men who kept the straining crowd at bay.

Despite the flash of cameras and volleys of shouts,

here in these few metres of space it was like being in the eye of a cyclone.

Instincts hyper-alert, Lucy surveyed the car the security men encircled. It was expensive, black with tinted windows.

Curious, she stepped forward, racking her brain. Her friends had melted away in these last years. As for her family—if only they could afford transport like this!

One of the bodyguards opened the back door and Lucy stepped close enough to look inside.

Grey eyes snared her. Eyes the colour of ice under a stormy sky. Sleek black eyebrows rayed up towards thick, dark hair cropped against a well-shaped head.

The clamour faded and Lucy's breath snagged as her eyes followed a long, arrogant nose, pinched as if in rejection of the institutional aroma she carried in her pores. High, angled cheekbones scored a patrician face. A solid jaw and a firm-set mouth, thinned beyond disapproving and into the realm of pained, completed a compelling face that might have stared out from a Renaissance portrait.

Despite the condemnation she read there, another emotion blasted between them, an unseen ripple of heat in the charged air. A ripple that drew her flesh tight and made the hairs on her arms rise.

'Domenico Volpe!'

Air hissed from Lucy's lungs as if from a puncture wound. Her hand tightened on her case and for a moment she rocked on her feet.

Not him! This was too much.

'You recognise me?' He spoke English with the clear, rounded vowels and perfect diction of a man with impeccable lineage, wealth, power and education at his disposal.

Which meant his disapproving tone, as if she had no right even to recognise a man so far beyond her league, was deliberate.

Lucy refused to let him see how that stung. Blank-faced withdrawal was a tactic she'd perfected as a defence in the face of aggression.

How could his words harm her after what she'd been through?

'I remember you.' *As if she could forget.* Once she'd almost believed… No. She excised the thought. She was no longer so foolishly naïve.

The sight of him evoked a volley of memories. She made herself concentrate on the later ones. 'You never missed a moment of the trial.'

The shouts of the crowd were a reminder of that time, twisting her insides with pain.

He didn't incline his head, didn't move, yet something flickered in his eyes. Something that made her wonder if he, like she, held onto control by a slim thread.

'Would you have? In my shoes?' His voice was silky but lethal. Lucy remembered reading that the royal assassins of the Ottoman sultan had used garrottes of silk to strangle their victims.

He wouldn't lower himself to assault but he wouldn't lift a finger to save her. Yet once long ago, for a fleeting moment, they'd shared something fragile and full of breathless promise.

Her throat tightened as memories swarmed.

What was she doing here, bandying words with a man who wished her only ill? Silently she turned but found her way blocked by a giant in a dark suit.

'Please, *signorina*.' He gestured to the open car door behind her. 'Take a seat.'

With Domenico Volpe? He personified everything that had gone wrong in her life.

A bubble of hysterical laughter rose and she shook her head.

She stepped to one side but the bodyguard moved fast. He grasped her arm, propelling her towards the car.

'Don't *touch* me!' All the shock and grief and dismay she battled rose within her, a roiling well of emotions she'd kept pent up too long.

No one had the right to coerce her.

Not any more.

Not after what she'd endured.

Lucy opened her mouth to demand her release. But the crisp, clear order she'd formulated didn't emerge. Instead a burst of Italian vitriol spilled out. Words she'd never known, even in English, till her time in jail. The sort of gutter Italian Domenico Volpe and his precious family wouldn't recognise. The sort of coarse, colloquial Italian favoured by criminals and lunatics. She should know, she'd met enough in her time.

The bodyguard's eyes widened, his hand dropping as he stepped back. As if he was afraid her lashing tongue might injure him.

Abruptly the flow of words stopped. Lucy vibrated with fury but also with something akin to shame.

So much for her pride in rising above the worst degradations of imprisonment. As for her pleasure, just minutes ago, that she'd left prison behind her… Her heart fell. How long would she bear its taint? How irrevocably had it changed her?

Despair threatened but she forced it down.

Fingers curling tight around the handle of her bag, she stepped forward and the bodyguard made way. She kept going, beyond the cordon that kept Domenico Volpe from the straining paparazzi.

Lucy straightened her spine. She'd rather walk into the arms of the waiting press than stay here.

'I'm sorry, boss. I should have stopped her. But with the media watching…'

'It's okay, Rocco. The last thing I want is a press report about us kidnapping Lucy Knight.' That would really send Pia into a spin. His sister-in-law was already strung out at the news of her release.

He watched the crowd close round the slim form of the Englishwoman and something that felt incredibly like remorse stirred.

As if he'd failed her.

Because she'd looked at him with unveiled horror and chosen the slavering mob rather than share a car with him? That niggling sense of guilt resurfaced. Nonsense, of course. In the light of day logic assured him she'd brought on her own destruction. Yet sometimes, in the dead of night, it didn't seem so cut and dried.

But he wasn't Lucy Knight's keeper. He never had been.

Five years ago he'd briefly responded to her air of fresh enthusiasm, so different from the sophisticated, savvy women in his life. Until he'd discovered she was a sham, trying to ensnare and use him as she had his brother.

Domenico's lips firmed. She'd looked at him just now with those huge eyes the colour of forget-me-nots. A gullible man might have read fear in that look.

Domenico wasn't a gullible man.

Though to his shame he'd felt a tug of unwanted attraction to the woman who'd stood day after day in the dock, projecting an air of bewildered innocence.

Her face had been a smooth oval, rounded with youth. Her hair, straight, long and the colour of wheat in the sun, had made him want to reach out and touch.

He'd hated himself for that.

'She's some wildcat, eh, boss? The way she let fly—'

'Close the door, Rocco.'

'Yes, sir.' The guard stiffened and shut the door.

Domenico sat back, watching the melee move down the street. A few stragglers remained, their cameras trained on the limousine, but the tinted windows gave privacy.

Just as well. He didn't want their lenses on him. Not when he felt...unsettled.

He swiped a hand over his jaw, wishing to hell

Pia hadn't put him in this situation. What did the media frenzy matter? They could rise above it as always. Only the insecure let the press get to them. But Pia was emotionally vulnerable, beset by mood swings and insecurities.

It wasn't the media that disturbed him. He ignored the paparazzi. It was *her*, Lucy Knight. The way she looked at him.

She'd changed. Her cropped hair made her look like a raunchy pixie instead of a soulful innocent. Her face had fined down, sculpted into bone-deep beauty that had been a mere promise at eighteen. And attitude! She had that in spades.

What courage had it taken to walk back into that hungry throng? Especially when he'd seen and heard, just for a moment, the pain in her hoarse curses.

For all the weeks of the trial she'd looked as if butter wouldn't melt in her mouth. How had she hidden such violent passion, such hatred so completely?

Or—the thought struck out of nowhere—maybe that dangerous undercurrent was something new, acquired in the intervening years.

Domenico sagged in his seat. He should ignore Pia's pleas and his own ambivalent reactions and walk away. This woman had been nothing but trouble since the day she'd crossed his family's threshold.

He pressed the intercom to speak to the driver. 'Drive on.'

Twenty minutes till the bus came.

Could she last? The crowd grew thicker. It took all Lucy's stamina to pretend they didn't bother her. To ignore the cameras and catcalls, the increasingly rough jostling.

Lucy's knees shook and her arm ached but she didn't dare put her case down. It held everything she owned and she wouldn't put it past one of the paparazzi to swipe it and do an exposé on the state of her underwear or a psychological profile based on the few battered books she possessed.

The tone of the gathering had darkened as the press found, instead of the easy prey they'd expected, a woman determined not to cooperate. Didn't they realise the last thing she wanted was more publicity?

They'd attracted onlookers. She heard their mutterings and cries of outrage.

She widened her stance, bracing against the pushing crowd, alert to the growing tension. She knew how quickly violence could erupt.

She was just about to give up on the bus and move

on when the crowd stirred. A flutter, like a sigh, rippled through it, leaving in its wake something that could almost pass for silence.

The camera crews parted. There, striding towards her was the man she'd expected never to see again: Domenico Volpe, shouldering through the rabble, eyes locked on her. He seemed oblivious to the snapping shutters as the cameras went into overdrive and newsmen gabbled into microphones.

He wore a grey suit with the slightest sheen, as if it were woven from black pearls. His shirt was pure white, his tie perfection in dark silk.

He looked the epitome of Italian wealth and breeding. Not a wrinkle marred his clothes or the elegant lines of his face. Only his eyes, boring into hers, spoke of something less than cool control.

A spike of heat plunged right through her belly as she held his eyes.

He stopped before her and Lucy had to force herself not to crane her head to look up at him. Instead she focused on the hand he held out to her.

The paper crackled as she took it.

Come with me. The words were in slashing black ink on a page from a pocketbook. *I can get you away from this. You'll be safe.*

Her head jerked up.

'Safe?' *With him?*

He nodded. 'Yes.'

Around them journalists craned to hear. One tried to snatch the note from Lucy's hand. She crumpled it in her fist.

It was mad. Bizarre. He couldn't want to help her. Yet she wasn't fool enough to think she could stay here. Trouble was brewing and she'd be at the centre of it.

Still she hesitated. This close, Lucy was aware of the strength in those broad shoulders, in that tall frame and his square olive-skinned hands. Once that blatant male power had left her breathless. Now it threatened.

But if he'd wanted to harm her physically he'd have found a way long before this.

He leaned forward. She stiffened as his whispered words caressed her cheek. 'Word of a Volpe.'

He withdrew, but only far enough to look her in the eye. He stood in her personal space, his lean body warming her and sending ripples of tension through her.

She knew he was proud. Haughty. Loyal. A powerful man. A dangerously clever one. But everything she'd read, and she'd read plenty, indicated he was a man of his word. He wouldn't sully his ancient family name or his pride by lying.

She hoped.

Jerkily she nodded.

'*Va bene.*' He eased the case from her white-knuckled grip and turned, propelling her through the crowd with his palm at her back, its heat searing through her clothes.

Questions rang out but Domenico Volpe ignored them. With his support Lucy rallied and managed not to stumble. Then suddenly there was blissful space, a cordon of security men, the open limousine door.

This time Lucy needed no urging. She scrambled in and settled herself on the far side of the wide rear seat.

The door shut behind him and the car accelerated away before she'd gathered herself.

'My bag!'

'It's in the boot. Quite safe.'

Safe. There it was again. The word she'd never associated with Domenico Volpe.

Slowly Lucy turned. She was exhausted, weary beyond imagining after less than an hour at the mercy of the paparazzi, but she couldn't relax, even in this decadently luxurious vehicle.

Deep-set grey eyes met hers. This time they looked stormy rather than glacial. Lucy was under no illusions that he wanted her here, with him. Despite the nonchalant stretch of his long legs, crossed at the ankles, there was tightness in his shoulders and jaw.

'What do you want?'

'To rescue you from the press.'

Lucy shook her head. 'No.'

'No?' One dark eyebrow shot up towards his hairline. 'You call me a liar?'

'If you'd been interested in rescuing me you'd have done it years ago when it mattered. But you dropped me like a hot potato.'

Her words sucked the oxygen from the limousine, leaving a heavy, clogging atmosphere of raw emotion. Lucy drew a deep breath, uncaring that he noted the agitated rise and fall of her breasts as she struggled for air.

'You're talking about two different things.' His tone was cool.

'You think?' She paused. 'You're playing semantics. The last thing you want is to *rescue* me.'

'Then let us say merely that your interests and mine coincide this time.'

'How?' She leaned forward, as if a closer view would reveal the secrets he kept behind that patrician façade of calm. 'I can't see what we have in common.'

He shook his head, turning more fully. Lucy became intensely aware of the strength hidden behind that tailored suit as his shoulders blocked her view of the street.

A jitter of curious sensation sped down her backbone and curled deep within. It disturbed her.

'Then you have an enviably short memory, Ms Knight. Even you can't deny we're linked by a tie that binds us forever, however much I wish it otherwise.'

'But that's—'

'In the past?' His lip curled in a travesty of a smile. 'Yet it's a truth I live with every day.' His eyes glowed, luminous with emotions she'd once thought him too cold to feel. His voice deepened to a low, bone-melting hum. 'Nothing will ever take away the fact that you killed my brother.'

CHAPTER TWO

LUCY KNIGHT SHOOK her head emphatically and for one crazy moment Domenico found himself mourning the fact that her blonde tresses no longer swirled round her shoulders. Why had she cut her hair so brutally short?

After *five years* he remembered how that curtain of silk had enticed him!

Impossible. It *wasn't* disappointment he felt.

He'd spent long days in court focused on the woman who'd stolen Sandro's life. He'd smothered grief, the urgent need for revenge and bone-deep disappointment that he'd got her so wrong. Domenico had forced himself to observe her every fleeting expression, every nuance. He'd imprinted her image in his mind.

Learning his enemy.

It wasn't attraction he'd felt then for the gold-digger who'd sought to play both the Volpe brothers. It had been clear-headed acknowledgement of her beauty and calculation of whether her little girl lost impression might prejudice the prosecution case.

'No. I was *convicted* of killing him. There's a difference.'

Domenico stared into her blazing eyes, alight with a passion that arrested logic. Then her words sank in, exploding into his consciousness like a grenade. His belly tightened as outrage flared.

He should have expected it. Yet to hear her voice the lie strained even his steely control.

'You're still asserting your innocence?'

Her eyes narrowed and her mouth tightened. Was she going to blast him with a volley of abuse as she had Rocco?

'Why wouldn't I? It's the truth.'

She held his gaze with a blatant challenge that made his hackles rise.

How dare she sit in the comfort of *his* car, talking about *his* brother's death, and deny all the evidence against her? Deny the testimony of Sandro's family and staff and the fair judgement of the court?

Bile surged in Domenico's throat. The gall of this woman!

'So you keep up the pretence. Why bother lying now?' His words rang with the condemnation he could no longer hide.

Meeting her outraged his sense of justice and sliced across his own inclinations. Only family duty compelled him to be here, conversing with his brother's killer. It revolted every one of his senses.

'This is no pretence, Signor Volpe. It's the truth.'

She leaned closer and he caught the scent of soap and warm female skin. His nostrils quivered, cataloguing a perfume that was more viscerally seductive than the lush designer scents of the women in his world.

'I did not kill your brother.'

She was some actress. Not even by a flicker did she betray her show of innocence.

That, above all, ignited his wrath. That she should continue this charade even now. Her dishonesty must run bone deep.

Or was she scared if she confessed he'd take justice into his own hands?

Domenico imagined his hands closing around that slim, pale throat, forcing her proud head back... but no. Rough justice held no appeal.

He wouldn't break the Volpe code of honour, even when provoked by this shameless liar.

'Now who's playing semantics? Sandro was off balance when you shoved him against the fireplace.' The words bit out from between clamped teeth. 'The knock to his head as he fell killed him.' Domenico drew in a slow breath, clawing back control. The men of his family did not give in to emotion. It was unthinkable he'd reveal to this woman the grief still haunting him.

'You were responsible. If he'd never met you he'd be alive today.'

Her face tightened and she swallowed. Remarkably he saw a flicker of something that might have been pain in her eyes.

Guilt? Regret for what she'd done?

An instant later that hint of vulnerability vanished.

Had he imagined it? Had his imagination supplied what he'd waited so long to see? Remorse over Sandro's death?

He catalogued the woman beside him. Rigid back, angled chin, hands folded neatly yet gripping too hard. Her eyes were different, he realised. After that first shocked expression of horror, now they were guarded.

The difference from the supposed innocent he'd met all those years ago was astounding. She'd certainly given up playing the ingénue.

She looked brittle. He sensed she directed all her energy into projecting that façade of calm.

Domenico knew it was a façade. Years of experience in the cutthroat world of business had made him an expert in body language. There was no mistaking the tension drawing her muscles tight or the short, choppy breaths she couldn't quite hide.

How much would it take to smash through to the real Lucy Knight? What would it take to make her crack?

'If you admitted the truth you'd find the future easier.'

'Why?' She tilted her head like a bright-eyed bird. 'Because confession is good for the soul?'

'So the experts say.'

He shifted into a more comfortable position as he awaited her response. Not by a flicker did he reveal how important this was to him.

Why, he didn't know. She'd already been proven guilty in a fair trial. Her guilt had been proclaimed to the world. But seeing her so defiant, Domenico faced an unpalatable truth. He realised with a certainty that ran deep as the blood he'd shared with his brother that this would never be over till Lucy Knight confessed.

Closure, truth, satisfaction, call it what you would. Only she could lay this to rest.

He hated her for the power that gave her.

'You think I'll be swayed by your attempts at psychology?' Her mouth curled in a hard little smile he'd never seen in all those weeks of the trial. 'You'll have to do better than that, Signor Volpe. If the experts couldn't extract a confession, you really think you will?'

'Experts?'

'Of course. You didn't think I was living in splendid isolation all this time, did you?' Her words sounded bitter but her expression remained unchanged. 'There's a whole industry around rehabilitating offenders. Didn't you know? Social workers, psychologists, psychiatrists.' She turned and looked out of the window, her profile serene.

Domenico fought the impulse to shake the truth from her.

'Did you know they assessed me to find out if I was insane?' She swung her head back around. Her face was blank but for the searing fire in her eyes. 'In case I wasn't fit to stand trial.' She paused. 'I suppose I was lucky. I can't recommend jail as a positive experience but I suspect an asylum for the criminally insane is worse. Just.'

Something passed between them. Some awareness, some connection, like a vibration in the taut air. Something that for a moment drew them together. It left Domenico unsettled.

Any connection with Lucy Knight was a betrayal of Sandro.

Anger snarled in his veins. 'You're alive to complain about your treatment. You didn't give my brother that option, did you? What you did was irrevocable.'

'And unpardonable. Is that why you spirited me away from the press? So you can berate me in private?'

She lounged back in her corner and made a production of crossing her legs as if to reinforce her total lack of concern. Even in her drab navy skirt and jacket there was no hiding the fact she had stunning legs. He was honest enough to admit it was one of the things that had drawn him the day they met. That and her shy smile. No wonder she'd always worn a skirt in court, trying to attract the male sympathy vote.

It hadn't worked then and it didn't work now.

'What a ripe imagination you have.' He let his teeth show in his slow smile and had the satisfaction of seeing her stiffen. 'I have better things to do with my time than talk with you.'

'In that case, you won't mind if I enjoy the view.' She turned to survey the street with an intense concentration he knew must be feigned.

Until he realised she hadn't seen anything like it for five years.

It was even harder than she'd expected being near Domenico Volpe. Sharing the same space. Talking with him.

A lifetime ago they'd shared a magical day, perfect in every way. By the time they'd parted with a promise to meet again she'd drifted on a cloud of delicious anticipation. He'd made her feel alive for the first time.

In a mere ten hours she'd fallen a little in love with her debonair stranger.

How *young* she'd been. Not just in years but experience. Looking back it was almost inconceivable she'd ever been that naïve.

When she'd seen him again it had been at her trial. Her heart had leapt, knowing he was there for her as she stood alone, battered by a world turned into nightmare. She'd waited day after day for him to break his silence, approach and offer a crumb of comfort. To look at her with warmth in his eyes again.

Instead he'd been a frowning dark angel come to exact retribution. He'd looked at her with eyes like winter, chilling her to the bone and shrivelling her dreams.

A shudder snaked through her but she repressed it. She was wrung out after facing the paparazzi and *him*, but refused to betray the fact that he got to her.

She should demand to know where they were headed, but facing him took all her energy.

Even his voice, low and liquid like rich dark chocolate laced with honey, affected her in ways she'd tried to suppress. It made her aware she was a healthy young woman programmed to respond to an attractive man. Despite his cold fury he made her aware of his masculinity.

Was it the vibration of his deep voice along her bones? His powerful male body? Or the supremely confident way he'd faced down the press as if he didn't give a damn what they printed? As if challenging them to take him on? All were too sexy for her peace of mind.

The way he looked at her disturbed, his scrutiny so intense it seemed he searched to find the real Lucy Knight. The one she'd finally learned to hide.

Lucy stifled a laugh. She'd been in prison too long. Maybe what she needed wasn't peace and quiet but a quick affair with an attractive stranger to get her rioting hormones under control.

The stranger filling her mind was Domenico Volpe.

No! That was wrong on so many levels her brain atrophied before she could go further.

She made herself concentrate on the street. No matter what pride said, it was a relief to be in the limo, whisked from the press in comfort.

Yet there'd be a reckoning. She'd given up believing in the milk of human kindness. There was a reason Domenico Volpe had taken her side. Something he wanted.

A confession?

Lucy pressed her lips together. He'd have a long wait. She'd never been a liar.

She was so wrapped in memories it took a while to realise the streets looked familiar. They drove through a part of Rome she knew.

Lucy straightened, tension trickling in a rivulet of ice water down her spine as she recognised landmarks. The shop where she'd found trinkets to send home to her dad and Sylvia, and especially the kids. The café that sold mouth-watering pastries to go with rich, aromatic coffee. The park where she'd taken little Taddeo under Bruno's watchful eye.

The trickle became a tide of foreboding as the limousine turned into an all too familiar street.

She swung around. Domenico Volpe watched her beneath lowered lids, his expression speculative.

'You can't be serious!' Her voice was a harsh scrape of sound.

'You wanted somewhere free from the press. They won't bother you here.'

'What do you call that?' The pavement before the Palazzo Volpe teemed with reporters. Beyond them the building rose, splendid and imposing, a monu-

ment to extreme wealth and powerful bloodlines.
A reminder of the disastrous past.

Lucy's heart plunged. She never wanted to see
the place again.

Was that his game? Retribution? Or did he think
returning her to the scene of the crime would force
a confession?

Nausea swirled as she watched the massive palazzo grow closer. Horror drenched her, leaving her
skin clammy as perspiration broke out beneath the
cloth of her suit.

'Stop the car!'

'Why? I wouldn't have thought you squeamish.'
His eyes were glacial again.

She opened her mouth to argue, then realised
there was no point. She'd been weak to go with
him and she had to face the consequences. Hadn't
she known he'd demand payment for his help?

Lucy lifted one shoulder in a shrug that cost her
every ounce of energy. 'I thought you wouldn't like
the press to know we were together. But on your
head be it. I've got nothing more to lose.'

'Haven't you?' His tone told her he'd make it his
business to find her soft spot and exploit it.

Let him try. He had no notion how a few years
in jail toughened a girl.

He fixed his gaze on her, not turning away as the

vehicle slowed to enter a well-guarded entrance. The crowd was held back by stony-faced security men. Anxiously Lucy scanned them but couldn't recognise any familiar faces.

Surreptitiously she let out a breath of relief.

Then the car slipped down a ramp. They entered a vast underground car park. A fleet of vehicles, polished to perfection, filled it. She saw limousines, a four wheel drive, a sleek motorbike and a couple of sports cars including a vintage one her dad would have given his eye teeth to drive.

Out of nowhere grief slammed into her. She'd missed him so long she'd finally learned to repress the waves of loss. But she hadn't been prepared for this.

Not now. Not here. Not in front of the man who saw himself as her enemy.

Maybe grief hit harder because it was her first day of freedom. The day, by rights, when she should be in her dad's reassuring embrace. But all that was gone. Lucy swallowed the knot of emotion clogging her throat, forcing herself to stare, dry-eyed, around the cavernous space.

'How did you get permission to excavate?' She was relieved her voice worked. 'I thought this part of the city was built on the ancient capital.'

'You didn't know about the basement car park?' His voice was sceptical.

Finally, when she knew her face was blank of emotion, Lucy met his stare. 'I was just the au pair, remember? Not the full-time nanny. I didn't go out with the family. Besides, Taddeo was so little and your sister-in-law—' she paused, seeing Domenico's gaze sharpen '—she didn't want him out and about. It was a struggle to get permission to take him to the park for air.'

Gun-metal grey eyes met hers and again she felt that curious beat of awareness between them. As if he knew and understood. But that was impossible. Domenico Volpe hated her, believed she'd killed his brother. Nothing would change his mind.

'The car park was necessary for our privacy.' His shoulders lifted in a shrug that indicated whatever the Volpe family needed the world would provide. *Naturally.* 'There was an archaeological survey but fortunately it didn't find anything precious.'

Lucy bit back a retort. It wouldn't matter how precious the remains. The Volpes would have got what they wanted. They always did. They'd wanted her convicted and they'd got their way.

The car slid to a halt and her door opened.

Lucy surveyed the big man holding it. Her heart gave a flip of relief as she saw it was the guy who'd tried to strong-arm her into the car earlier. Not a spectre from the past. But embarrassment warred with relief as she recalled how she'd abused him.

'Thank you.' She slid awkwardly from the seat, not used to a skirt after years in regulation issue trousers.

Silently he inclined his head.

Damp palms swiping down her skirt, Lucy located the rest of the security staff. Her heart clenched as she thought she saw a familiar figure in the dim light but when he moved Lucy realised it was another stranger. Her breathing eased.

'This way, *signorina*.' The bodyguard ushered her towards a lift.

Minutes later she found herself in a part of the palazzo she'd never visited. But its grand dimensions, its exquisitely intricate marble flooring and air of otherworld luxury were instantly familiar.

Her skin prickled as she inhaled that almost forgotten scent. Of furniture polish, hothouse flowers and, she'd once joked, money. Memories washed over her, of those first exciting days in a new country, of her awe at her surroundings, of that last night—

'Ms Knight?' *Lucy*, he'd called her once. For a few bright, brief hours. Instantly Domenico slammed the memory of that folly into an iron vault of memory.

She spun around and he saw huge, haunted eyes. Her face had paled and her fine features were pinched.

The mask slipped at last.

He should feel satisfaction at her unease in his family home. But it wasn't pleasure he experienced. He had no name for this hyper-awareness, this knife-edge between antipathy and absorption.

Sensation feathered through him, like the tickle of his conscience, teasing him for bringing her here.

Lucy Knight had fascinated him all those years ago. To his chagrin he realised she still did. More than was desirable. It was one thing to know your enemy. Another to respond to her fear with what felt too much like sympathy.

As he watched the moment of vulnerability was gone. Her face smoothed out and her pale eyebrows arched high as if waiting for him to continue.

'This way.' He gestured for her to accompany him, conscious of her beside him as they headed to his side of the palazzo. She was a head shorter but kept pace easily, not hesitating for a moment.

He had to hand it to her; she projected an air of assurance many of his business associates would envy. Twice now he'd seen behind the façade of calm but both times it had been a quick glimpse and the circumstances had been enough to discomfit anyone.

In his study he gestured for her to take a seat. Instead she prowled the room, inspecting the bookcases, the view from the window and, he was sure, scoping out a possible escape route. There was none.

Instead of taking one of the sofas near the fireplace as he'd intended, Domenico settled behind his desk.

'Why have you brought me here?'

She stood directly before the desk, feet planted as if to ground herself ready for attack.

'To talk.'

'Talk?' The word shot out. 'You had your chance to talk five years ago. As I recall, you weren't interested in renewing our acquaintance.' Her tone was bitter and her eyes glittered with fury.

The difference between this Amazon and the girl he'd briefly known struck him anew.

'And to separate you and the press.'

'No altruistic rescue then.' She gave no indication of disappointment, merely met his gaze in frank appraisal.

'Did you expect one?'

'No.' She answered before he'd finished speaking.

Why did her readiness to distrust rankle? He hadn't expected doe-eyed innocence. The scales had been ripped from his eyes long ago.

'Feel free to sit.'

'No.' She paused. 'Thank you. I prefer to stand.' She swallowed hard.

Thanking him must almost have choked her.

As having her in his home revolted every sensibility. Was Sandro turning in his grave? No. Sandro would have approved of his actions.

'For how long?' She watched him closely.

'As long as it takes.'

She frowned. 'As long as what takes?'

Domenico leaned back in his chair. He sensed it was too early to reveal his full intent. Better proceed slowly than rush and have her refuse out of hand.

'For the press to lose interest in this story.'

'There *is* no story. It happened so long ago.'

Domenico's belly clenched. 'You think what happened means nothing now? That it's all over?'

Her head shot up. 'It *is* over. I've served the sentence for manslaughter and now I'm free. If there was anything I could do to bring your brother back I would.' She heaved a deep breath that strained her breasts against the dark fabric. 'But there's not.'

'You cut off my brother's life in his prime.' Anger

vibrated in his words and he strove to modulate his voice. 'You made my sister-in-law a widow before her time. She was barely a wife, still struggling to adapt to motherhood, and suddenly she was alone.'

Sky blue eyes met his unflinchingly.

Did none of it matter to her?

'Because of you my nephew will never know his father.' The words grated from a throat scraped raw with anger. 'You denied them both that. You left a gaping hole in his life.'

As she'd ripped a hole in Domenico's life. Even now he found it hard to believe Sandro was gone. The older brother who'd been his friend, his pillar of strength when their parents had died and Domenico was still a kid. His mentor, who'd applauded his tenacity when he'd branched out as an entrepreneur, building rather than relying on the family fortune and traditions.

He wanted her to know the pain she'd caused. To *feel* it. The civilised man he was knew she'd paid the price society saw fit for her crime. The wounded, grief-stricken one wanted more. Remorse. Guilt. A confession. *Something.*

'You can't control the press.' She spoke as if nothing he'd said mattered, brushing aside so much pain.

For a full thirty seconds Domenico stared at the woman who'd destroyed so much, yet felt so little.

He couldn't understand how anyone could be so devoid of compassion. He wished he'd never sullied himself by helping her, even if it wasn't for her benefit.

But he refused to let Sandro's family suffer any more because of Lucy Knight.

'I can starve them of fresh news.'

'But there *is* no news.'

'You're out of jail. The murderess set free.'

Her chin jutted. 'The charge was manslaughter.'

Domenico bit down the need to tell her legalistic quibbling didn't change the fact of Sandro's death. Instead he reached for the glossy pages on his desk.

'There's still a story. Especially after this.'

'What is it?' She stepped forward, her expression closed, but he read the rigidity of her slim frame, as if she prepared for the worst.

For a second Domenico hesitated. Why, he didn't know. Then he tossed the magazine across the gleaming surface of the desk.

She tilted her head to read it where it lay, as if not wanting to touch it. He couldn't blame her. It was the sort of trash he avoided, but Pia, his sister-in-law, was obviously a fan. She'd brought it to his attention, hysterical that the sordid tragedy was being resurrected.

Eventually Lucy Knight reached out and flipped

the page with one finger. The story spread across both pages. Her likeness featured beside the text. Another picture of her and an older man, her father. Then more of a rather hollow-eyed woman and a gaggle of children.

He watched Lucy Knight's eyes widen, heard her breath hitch, then a hiss of shock. She'd turned the colour of ash. Even her lips paled. Rapidly she blinked and he could have sworn tears welled in those remarkable eyes.

Then, with a suddenness that caught him off guard, the woman he'd thought as unfeeling as an automaton swayed off balance and he realised she was going to faint.

CHAPTER THREE

LUCY STARED AS the text blurred and dipped. She blinked, torn between gratitude that she couldn't make out all the snide character assassination and desperation to know the worst.

She thought she'd experienced the worst in prison. With the loss of her father, her friends, freedom, innocence and self-esteem.

She'd been wrong.

This was the final betrayal.

She struggled to draw breath. It was as if a boulder squashed her lungs. She slammed a hand on the satiny wood of the desk, her damp palm slipping as she fought to steady herself.

Darkness rimmed her vision and the world revolved, churning sickeningly like a merry-go-round spinning off kilter.

There was a pounding in her ears and a gaping hole where her heart had been.

Hard fingers closed around her upper arm.

It was enough to drag her back to her surroundings. She yanked her arm but the grip tightened. She felt him beside her, imprisoning her against the desk.

From somewhere deep inside fury welled, a volcanic force that for a glorious moment obliterated the pain shredding her vitals.

Driven by unstoppable instinct Lucy pivoted, raised her hand and chopped down on the inner elbow of the arm that captured her. At the same time she jabbed her knee high in his groin. Her hand connected with a force that almost matched the strength in that muscled arm. But her knee struck only solid thigh as he sensed her attack and shifted.

Yet it worked. She was free. She stood facing him, panting from adrenalin and overflowing emotions.

Gimlet eyes stared down at her. Glittering eyes that bored deep into her soul, as if he could strip away the self-protective layers she'd built so painstakingly around herself and discover the woman no one else knew.

Her chest rose and fell as she struggled for air. Her pulse thundered. Her skin sizzled with the effervescence in her bloodstream.

The muzzy giddiness disappeared as she stared back at the face of the man who'd stripped away

her last hope and destroyed what was left of her
joy at being free.

Far from fainting, she felt painfully alive. It was
as if layers of skin had been scored away, exposing nerve endings that throbbed from contact with
the very air in this cloistered mansion.

'Don't touch me!'

Instead of backing off from her snarling tone he
merely narrowed his eyes.

'You were going to faint.' The rumble of his voice
stirred an echo inside her.

'I've never fainted in my life.' She shoved aside
the knowledge that he was right. Until the shock of
his touch she'd been about to topple onto his pris-
tine parquet floor.

'You needed support.' His words betrayed no outrage at her attack. It was as if he, like she, was no
longer bothered by social niceties. As if he understood the primitive intensity of her feelings.

That disturbed her. She didn't want him understanding anything about her. She didn't like the
sense that Domenico Volpe had burrowed under
her skin and was privy to her innermost demons.

Something shifted in his gaze. There was a subtle
difference in those deep-set eyes that now shone
silver. Something in the line of his lips. Her eyes

lingered there, tracing the shape of a mouth which now, relaxed, seemed designed solely for sensual pleasure.

A gossamer thread of heat spun from her breasts to her pelvis, drawing tight—a heat she'd felt only once before.

Had his expression changed, grown warm? Or had something inside her shifted?

Lucy bit her lip then regretted the movement as his gaze zeroed in on her mouth. Her lips tingled as if he'd reached out and grazed them with a questing finger.

A shiver of luxurious pleasure ripped through her. Fire ignited deep within, so hot it felt as if she were melting. Her pulse slowed to a ponderous beat then revved out of control.

She'd known Domenico Volpe was dangerous. But she hadn't known the half of it.

She swallowed hard and found her voice, trying to ignore her body's flagrant response.

'You can move back now. I can stand.'

He took his time moving. 'Yet sitting is so much more comfortable, don't you think?'

He said no more but that one raised eyebrow told her he saw what she'd rather not reveal. That her surge of energy was short-lived. Lucy felt a dragging at her limbs. Her knees were jelly and the thought of confronting him here, now, was almost too much to bear.

Had he guessed her visceral response to his flagrant masculinity? That would be the final straw.

She grabbed the magazine, crushing its pages.

'Thank you. I will take that seat now.'

He nodded and gestured to a long sofa. Instead she took the black leather swivel chair that looked like something from an exclusive design catalogue, a far cry from the sparse utilitarian furniture she'd grown used to. It was wickedly comfortable and her bones melted as she sank into it. It was massive, built to order, she guessed, for the man who took a seat across from her. Lucy tried to look unfazed by such luxury.

'You didn't know about the article?'

Lucy refused to look away from his keen gaze. Confrontation was preferable to running. She'd learned that in a hard school. But looking him in the eye was difficult when her body hummed with the aftermath of what she could only describe as an explosion of sexual awareness.

'No.' She glanced down at the trashy gossip mag and repressed a shiver. It was like holding a venomous snake in her palm. 'I had no idea.'

'Would you like something? Brandy? A pot of tea?'

Startled by his concern, she turned to find Domenico Volpe looking almost as surprised as she was, as if the offer had slipped out without volition.

It was no comfort to know she must look as bad as she felt for him to offer sustenance.

'No. Thank you.' Accepting anything from him went against every instinct.

Already he moved towards the desk. Obviously it didn't matter what she wanted. 'I'll order coffee.'

Lucy's gaze dropped to the magazine. How could Sylvia have done this? Did she despise Lucy so much?

Silently her heart keened. Sylvia and the kids had been Lucy's last bright hope of returning to some remnant of her old life. Of having family again. Of belonging.

Quotes from the article floated through her troubled mind. Of her stepmother saying Lucy had 'always been *different*', 'withdrawn and moody' but 'hankering after the bright lights and excitement'. That she put her own needs first rather than those of her family. There was nothing in the article about Sylvia's resentment of her husband's almost grown daughter, or the fact that Lucy had spent years as unpaid nurserymaid for Sylvia's four children by a previous marriage. Or that Sylvia's idea of bright lights was a Saturday night in Torquay and a take-away meal.

Nothing about the fact that Lucy had left home only when her dad, in his quiet way, had urged her to experience more of the world rather than put her life on hold to look after the younger children.

She'd experienced the world all right, but not in the way he'd had in mind.

As for the article, taken from a recent interview with Sylvia, it was a lurid exposé that painted Lucy as an uncaring, amoral gold-digger. It backed up every smear and innuendo that had been aired in the courtroom. Worse, it proved even her family had turned against her.

What would her stepsiblings think now they were old enough to read such malicious gossip?

Lucy's heart withered and she pressed a hand to her throat, trying to repress rising nausea. Sylvia and she had never been close but Lucy had never thought her stepmother would betray her like this. The article's spitefulness stole her breath.

Until now she'd believed there was someone believing in her. First her father and, after he died, Sylvia.

She felt bereft, grieving all over again for her dad who'd been steadfastly behind her. Never having known her long-dead mother, Lucy's bond with her father had been special. His faith and love had kept her strong through the trial.

Lucy had never been so alone. Not even that first night in custody. Even after the conviction when she knew she had years of imprisonment ahead. Nor facing down the taunts and jeers as she'd learned to handle the threats from prisoners who'd tried to make her life hell.

The magazine was a rag but an upmarket one. Sylvia had sold her out for what must be a hefty fee.

Lucy blinked stinging eyes as she stared at the vile publication in her lap.

She thought she'd known degradation and despair. But it was only now that her life hit rock bottom.

And Domenico Volpe was here to see it.

She shivered, chilled to the marrow. How he must be gloating.

'The coffee will be here soon.'

Lucy looked up to find him standing across from her, watchful. No doubt triumphing at the sight of her down and out. Framed by the massive antique fireplace and a solid wall of books, he looked the epitome of born and bred privilege. From his aristocratically handsome features to his hand stitched shoes he screamed power and perfection.

Once the sight of him had made her heart skip

with pleasure. But she'd discovered the real Domenico Volpe when the chips were down. He'd sided with his own class, easily believing the most monstrous lies against her.

Slowly she stood, pride stiffening her weary legs and tilting her chin.

'It's time I left.'

Where she'd go she had no idea, but she had to escape.

She had just enough money to get her home to Devon. But now she had no home. Her breath hitched as she thought of Sylvia's betrayal. She wouldn't be welcome there.

Pain transfixed her.

'You can't leave.'

'I'm now officially a free woman, Signor Volpe, however much you resent it. If you try to keep my here by force it will be kidnap.'

Even so a shiver of apprehension skated down her spine. She wouldn't put anything past him. She'd seen his cadre of security men and she knew first hand what they were capable of.

'You mistake me for one of your recent associates, Ms Knight.' He snapped the words out as if he wanted to take a bite out of her. 'I've no intention of breaking the law.'

Before she could voice her indignation he continued. 'You need somewhere private; somewhere the press can't bother you.'

His words stilled her protest.

'And?'

'I can provide that place.'

And pigs might fly.

'Why would you do that?' She'd read his contempt. 'What do you get out of it?'

For the longest moment he stood silent. Only the hint of a scowl on his autocratic features hinted he wasn't used to being questioned. Tough.

'There are others involved,' he said finally. 'My brother's widow and little Taddeo. They're the ones affected the longer this is dragged through the press.'

Taddeo. Lucy had thought of him often. She'd loved the little baby in her care, enjoying his gurgles of delight at their peekaboo games and his wide-eyed fascination as she'd read him picture books. What was he like now?

One look at Domenico Volpe's closed face told her he'd rather walk barefoot over hot coals than talk about his nephew with her.

'So what's your solution?' She crossed her arms over her chest. 'Walling me up in the basement car park?'

'That could work.' He bared his teeth in a feral

smile that drew her skin tight. 'But I prefer to work within the law.' He paused. 'I don't have your penchant for the dramatic. Instead I suggest providing you with a bolthole till this blows over. Your bag is already in your room.'

Her room.

Lucy groped for the back of the chair she'd just vacated, her hand curling like a claw into the plump, soft leather. She tried to speak but her voice had dried up.

Her room.

The memory of it had haunted her for years. Ever since arriving here she'd been cold to the core because she knew that room was upstairs, on the far side of the building.

'You can't expect me to stay there!' Her voice was hoarse with shock. 'Even *you* couldn't…' She shook her head as her larynx froze. 'That's beyond cruel. That's *sick.*'

His eyes widened and she saw understanding dawn. His nostrils flared and he stepped towards her, then pulled up abruptly.

'No.' The word slashed the clogged silence. 'That room hasn't been used since my brother died. There's another guest room at your disposal.'

Relief sucked her breath away and loosened her

cramped muscles. Slowly she drew in oxygen, marshalling all her strength to regroup after that scare.

'I can't stay in this house.'

He met her gaze silently, not asking why. He knew. The memories were too overwhelming.

'I'll find my own place.'

'And how will you do that with the press on the doorstep?' He crossed his arms over his chest and leaned a shoulder against the fireplace, projecting an air of insouciance that made her want to slap him. 'Wherever you go they'll follow. You'll get no peace, no privacy.'

He was right, damn him. But to be dependent on him for anything stuck in her craw.

The door opened and a maid entered, bearing a tray of coffee and biscuits. The rich aroma, once her favourite, curdled Lucy's stomach. Instinctively she pressed a hand to her roiling abdomen and moved away. Vaguely she heard him thank the maid, but from her new vantage point near the window Lucy saw only the press pack outside. The blood leached from her cheeks.

Which was worse? Domenico Volpe or the paparazzi who'd hound her for some tawdry story they could sell?

'If you don't mind, I'll take you up on the offer of

that room. Just to freshen up.' She needed breathing space, time away from him, to work out what to do.

Lucy swung round to find him watching her. She should be used to it now. His scrutiny was continual. Yet reaction shivered through her. What did he see? How much of what she strove to hide?

She banished the question. She had better things to do than worry about that. Nothing would change Domenico Volpe's opinion. His reluctant gestures of solicitude were evidence of ingrained social skills, not genuine concern.

'Of course. Take as long as you like. Maria will show you up.'

Lucy assured herself it wasn't satisfaction she saw in that gleaming gaze.

'No! I said I can't talk. I'm busy.' Sylvia's voice rose and Lucy thought she discerned something like anxiety as well as anger in her stepmother's words. She gripped the phone tighter.

'I just wanted—'

'Well, I *don't* want. Just leave me alone! Haven't you done enough damage to this family?'

Lucy opened her mouth but the line went dead.

How long she sat listening to the dialling tone she didn't know. When she finally put the receiver down her fingers were cramped and her shoulders stiff from hunching, one arm wrapped protectively around her stomach.

So that was it. The severing of all ties.

A piercing wail of grief rose inside her but she stifled it. Lucy told herself it was better to face this now than on the rose-covered doorstep of the white-washed cottage that had been home all her life.

Yet she couldn't quite believe it. She'd rung her stepmother hoping against hope there'd been some dreadful mistake. That perhaps the press had published a story with no basis. That Sylvia hadn't betrayed her with that character assassination interview.

Forlorn hope! Sylvia wanted nothing to do with her.

Which left Lucy with nowhere to go. She had no one and nothing but a past that haunted her and even now wouldn't release its awful grip.

Slowly she lifted her head and stared at the panelled door separating the bedroom from the second-floor corridor.

It was time she laid the ghost of her past to rest.

She wasn't in the room he'd provided but she hadn't tried to leave. His security staff would have alerted him. There was only one place she could be, yet he hadn't thought she'd have the gall to go back there.

Domenico's stride lengthened as he paced the corridor towards the side of the palazzo that had housed Sandro's apartments. Fury spiked as he thought of Lucy Knight there, in the room where she'd taken Sandro's life. It was an intrusion that proved her contempt for all he and his family had lost. A trespass that made his blood boil and his body yearn for violence.

The door was open and he marched across the threshold, hands clenched in iron fists, muscles taut and fire in his belly.

Then he saw her and stopped dead.

He didn't know what he'd expected but it wasn't this. Lucy Knight was huddled on the floor before the ornate fireplace, palm pressed to the floorboards where Sandro had breathed his last. Domenico remembered it from the police markers on the floor and photos in court.

Her face was the colour of travertine marble, pale beyond belief. Her eyes were dark with pain as she stared fixedly before her. She was looking at something he couldn't see, something that shuttered her gaze and turned it inwards.

The hair prickled at his nape and he stepped further into the room.

She looked up and shock slammed him at the anguish he saw in her face. Gone was the sassy, prickly woman who'd fought him off when he'd dared touch her.

The woman before him bore the scars of bone-deep pain. It was clear in every feature, so raw he almost turned away, as if seeing such emotion was a violation.

A shudder passed through him. Shock that instead of the anger he'd nursed as he strode through the house, it was something like pity that stirred.

'I'm sorry.' Her voice was a rasp of laboured air. 'It shouldn't have happened. I was so young and stupid.' Her voice faded as she looked down at the patina of old wood beneath her hands. 'I should never have let him in.'

Domenico crossed the room in a few quick strides and hunkered beside her, his heart thumping.

She admitted it?

It didn't seem possible after all this time.

'If I hadn't let him in, none of it would have happened.' She drew a breath that shook her frame. 'I've gone over it so often. If only I hadn't listened to him. If only I'd locked the door.'

Domenico frowned. 'You had no need to lock the door against my brother. I refuse to believe he would have forced himself on you.'

The idea went against everything he knew about Sandro. His brother had been a decent man. A little foolish in his choice of wife, but honourable. A loving brother and doting father. A man who'd made one mistake, led astray by a beautiful, scheming seductress, but *not* a man who took advantage of female servants.

That blonde head swung towards him and she blinked. 'I wasn't talking about your brother. I was talking about the bodyguard, Bruno.' Her voice slowed on the name as if her tongue thickened. Domenico heard what sounded like fear in her voice. 'I shouldn't have let Bruno in.'

Domenico shot to his feet. Disappointment was so strong he tasted it, a rusty tang, on his tongue.

'You still stick to that story?'

The bruised look in her eyes faded, replaced by familiar wariness. Her mouth tightened and for an instant Domenico felt a pang almost of loss as she donned her habitual air of challenge.

A moment later she was again that woman ready to defy the world with complete disdain. Even curled up at his feet she radiated a dignity and inner strength he couldn't deny.

How did she do it? And why did he let it get to him? She was a liar and a criminal, yet there was something about her that made him wish things were different.

There always had been. *That was the hell of it.*

His gut dived. Even to think it was a betrayal of Sandro.

'I don't tell stories, Signor Volpe.' She got to her feet in a supple movement that told him she hadn't spent the last years idle. 'Bruno killed your brother but—' she raised her hand when he went to speak '—don't worry, you won't hear it from me again. I'm tired of repeating myself to people who won't listen.'

She made to move past him but his hand shot out to encircle her upper arm. Instantly she tensed. Would she try to fight him off as she had downstairs? He almost wished she would. There'd be a primitive satisfaction in curbing her temper and stamping his control on that fiery, passionate nature she hid behind the untouchable façade.

Heat tingled through his fingers where he held her. He braced himself but she merely looked at him, eyebrows arching.

'You wanted something?' Acid dripped from her words.

Domenico's eyes dropped to her mouth, soft pink again now that colour had returned to her face. The blush pink of rose petals at dawn.

A pulse of something like need thudded through his chest. He told himself it was the urge to wring her pretty neck. Yet his mouth dried when he watched her lips part a fraction, as if she had trouble inhaling enough air. There was a buzzing in his ears.

Her eyes widened and Domenico realised he'd leaned closer. Too close. Abruptly he straightened, dropping her arm as if it burnt him.

'I want to know what you plan to do.'

He didn't have the right to demand it. Her glittering azure gaze told him that. But he didn't care. She wasn't the only one affected by this media frenzy. He had family to protect.

'I want to find somewhere private, away from the news hounds.'

He nodded. 'I can arrange that.'

'Not here!' The words shot out. A frisson shuddered through the air, a reminder of shadows from the past.

'No, not here.' He had estates in Italy as well as in California's Napa Valley and another outside London. Any of them would make a suitable safe house till this blew over.

'In that case, I accept your generous offer, Signor Volpe. I'll stay in your safe haven for a week or so, until this furore dies down.'

She must be more desperate than she appeared. She hadn't even asked where she'd be staying. Or with whom.

CHAPTER FOUR

LUCY WOKE TO silence.

Cocooned in a wide comfortable bed with crisp cotton sheets and the fluffiest of down pillows, she lay, breathing in the sense of peace.

She felt…safe.

The realisation sideswiped her.

Who'd have thought she'd owe Domenico Volpe such a debt? A solid night's sleep, undisturbed till late morning judging by the sunlight rimming the curtains. She couldn't remember the last time she'd slept so long or so soundly.

Lucy flung back the covers, eager to see where she was. Last night she'd left from the helipad on the roof of the palazzo and headed into darkness. Domenico Volpe had said merely she'd go to one of his estates, somewhere she could be safe from press intrusion.

After yesterday's traumas that had been good enough for her. She desperately needed time to lick her wounds and decide what to do. With no friends, no job and very little money the outlook was grim.

Till she pulled back the curtains and gasped. Strong sunlight made her blink as she took in a vista of wide sky, sea and a white sand beach below a manicured garden.

It was paradise. The garden had an emerald lawn, shade trees and sculpted hedges. Pots of pelargoniums and other plants she couldn't identify spilled a profusion of flowers in a riot of colours, vivid against the indigo sea.

Unlatching the sliding glass door, Lucy stepped onto a balcony. Warmth enveloped her and the scent of growing things. Birds sang and she heard, like the soft breath of a sleeping giant, the gentle shush of waves. Dazzled, she stared, trying to absorb it all. But her senses were overloaded. Tranquillity and beauty surrounded her and absurdly she felt the pinprick of hot tears.

She'd dreamed of freedom but had never imagined a place like this. Her hands clenched on the railing. It was almost too much to take in. Too much change from the grey, authoritarian world she'd known.

A moment later she'd scooped up a cotton robe and dragged it on over her shabby nightgown. She cinched the tie at her waist as she pattered down the spiral staircase from her balcony.

Reflected light caught her eye and she spied a huge infinity pool that seemed to merge with the sea beyond. Turf cushioned her bare feet as she made for the balustrade overlooking the sea. Yet she stopped time and again, admiring an arbour draped with scented flowers, a pool that reflected the sprawling villa, unexpected groves and modern sculptures.

'Who are you? I'm Chiara and I'm six.' The girl's Italian had a slight lisp.

Lucy turned to meet inquisitive dark eyes and a sunny smile. Automatically her lips curved in response to the girl's gap-toothed grin, stretching facial muscles Lucy hadn't used in what seemed a lifetime.

'I'm Lucy and I'm twenty-four.'

'That's so old.' The little girl paused, looking up from her hidey-hole behind a couple of palm trees. 'Don't you wish you were six too?'

Unfamiliar warmth spread through Lucy. 'Today I do.' How wonderful to enjoy all this without a care for the future that loomed so empty.

It had been years since she'd seen a child, much less talked with one. Looking into that dimpled face, alight with curiosity, she realised how much she'd missed. If things had been different she'd have spent her life working with children. Once she had the money behind her to study, she'd intended to train as a teacher.

But her criminal record made that impossible.

'Will you play with me?'

Lucy stiffened. Who would want her daughter playing with an ex-con? A woman with her record?

'You'd better talk to your mummy first. You shouldn't play with strangers, you know.'

The little girl's eyes widened. 'But you're not a stranger. You're a friend of Domi's, aren't you?'

'Domi?' Lucy frowned. 'I don't know—'

'This is his house.' Chiara spread her hands wide. 'The house and garden. The whole island.'

'I see. But I still can't play with you unless your mummy says it's all right.'

'Uncle Rocco!' The little girl spoke to someone behind Lucy. 'Can I play with Lucy? She says I can't unless Mummy says so but Mummy's away.'

Lucy spun round to see the stolid face of the big security guard she'd lambasted outside the prison. Did it have to be him of all people? Heat flushed her skin but she held his gaze till he turned to the little girl, his features softening.

'That's for Nonna to decide. But it can't be today. Signorina Knight just arrived. You can't bother her with your chatter.' He took the child by the hand and, with a nod at Lucy, led her to the villa.

Lucy turned towards the sea. Still beautiful, it had lost some of its sparkle.

At least Rocco hadn't betrayed his horror at finding his niece with a violent criminal. But he'd hurried to remove her from Lucy's tainted presence.

Pain jagged her chest, robbing her of air. Predictable as his reaction was, she couldn't watch them leave. Her chest clamped around her bruised heart and she sagged against the stone balustrade.

Lucy had toughened up years ago. The naïve innocent was gone, replaced by a woman who viewed the world with cynicism and distrust. A woman who didn't let the world or life get to her any more.

Yet the last twenty-four hours had been a revelation.

She'd confronted the paparazzi, then Domenico Volpe, learnt of Sylvia's betrayal and faced the place where her life had changed irrevocably. Now she confronted a man's instinct to protect his niece, from *her*.

All tore at her precious self-possession. It had taken heartache, determination and hard-won strength to build the barriers that protected her. She'd been determined never to experience again those depths of terror and pain of her first years in prison. Until now those barriers had kept her strong and safe.

Who'd have thought she still had the capacity to hurt so much?

She leant on the railing, eyes fixed on the south Italian mainland in the distance.

Domenico took in her slumped shoulders and the curve of her arms around her body, hugging out a hostile world.

It reminded him of the anguish he thought he'd spied yesterday in her old room at the palazzo. She'd hunched like a wounded animal over the spot Sandro had died. The sight had poleaxed him, playing on protective instincts he'd never expected to feel around her.

Almost, he'd been convinced by that look of blind pain in her unfocused eyes. But she'd soon disabused him. It had been an act, shrewd and deliberate, to con him into believing her story of innocence.

Innocent? The woman who'd seduced his brother then killed him?

He'd once fancied he felt a connection with the girl who'd burst like pure sunshine into his world. But before he could fall completely under her spell tragedy and harsh truth had intervened, revealing her true colours.

A breeze flirted with her wrap, shifting it against the curve of her hip and bottom.

She didn't look innocent.

He remembered her trial. The evidence of Sandro's Head of Security and of Pia, Sandro's widow, that Lucy Knight had deliberately played up to Sandro, flirting and ultimately seducing him.

When it became clear her relationship with Sandro was core to the case against her, Lucy Knight had offered to have a medical test proving her virginity.

You could have heard a pin drop in the courtroom as all eyes fixed on her nubile body and wide, seemingly innocent eyes. Every man in that room had wondered about the possibility of being her first. *Even Domenico.*

The prosecution had successfully argued it was her intentions that mattered, not whether the affair had yet been consummated. In the end a medical test was deemed immaterial but for a while she'd cleverly won sympathy, despite the rest of the evidence.

Having seen her in action, Domenico had no doubt she knew exactly how to seduce even the most cautious man.

He traced the shapely line of her legs down to her bare feet and something thudded in his chest. Was the rest of her bare beneath that wrap?

His body tightened from chest to groin as adrenalin surged. His pulse thudded. Physical awareness saturated him and he cursed under his breath.

Hunger for Lucy Knight was *not* to be contemplated.

Yet the hectic drumming in his blood didn't abate.

As if sensing him, she turned her head. 'You! What are you doing here?' She spun to face him, legs planted wide and hands clenched at her sides, a model of aggressive challenge.

Except for the robe's gaping neckline and the flutter of cotton around bare thighs that highlighted her femininity.

Domenico reminded himself he liked his women accommodating. Soft and pliant. Warrior queens with lofty chins and defiance in every sinew held no appeal.

Till now.

His body's wayward response angered him and guilt pricked. This woman had destroyed Sandro.

'This is my property. Or had you forgotten?'

'You implied I'd be here alone.'

'Did I? Are you sure?' Of course she wasn't. He'd chosen his words carefully. Even to his enemies,

Domenico didn't lie. Seeing her skittishness, he'd deliberately neglected to mention he'd arrive here today. 'I fail to see what my travel plans have to do with you.'

He waited for her to splutter her indignation. But she merely surveyed him through slitted eyes. He sensed she drew her defences tight, preparing for battle.

Was she like this with everyone or just him?

'You came to make sure I don't steal the silver.' The sarcastic jibe almost hid her curiously flat tone. Yet he heard that hint of suppressed emotion, as if she was genuinely disappointed.

As if what he thought mattered.

Domenico frowned, instinct and intellect warring. He *knew* what she was, yet when he looked at her he *felt*…

Abruptly she pulled her robe in tight, as if only now realising the loose front revealed the shadow of her cleavage. Methodically she knotted the belt, all the while holding his gaze. Why did it feel as if she were putting on armour, rather than merely covering herself?

Did she know, with the light behind her, the wrap revealed rather than concealed her curves? Was it a deliberate ploy to distract him?

His voice was harsh. 'I leave it to my security staff to watch for thieves.'

Did she flinch? He remembered her rosy flush in court when evidence had been presented about the jewellery she'd either been given or had stolen from Sandro.

No sign of a blush now.

'What do you want?' Her insolence made his hackles rise.

It was on the tip of his tongue to deny he wanted anything, but pragmatism beat pride. He was here for one reason only and the sooner he fixed it the sooner he could put Lucy Knight firmly in the past.

'I do have some business to discuss with you but—'

'Ha! I knew it!' She folded her arms and Domenico had to force his gaze above the plump swell of her breasts, accentuated by the gesture.

'Knew what?' To his chagrin he'd missed something. He who never missed a nuance of any business negotiation.

'That it was too good to be true.' Her lip curled. 'No one gives anything for nothing. Especially you.' Her gaze flicked him from head to toe as if she read his body's charged response to her. His skin drew tight. Fury spilled and pooled. At her dismissive tone. At himself for the spark of arousal he couldn't douse.

'You're here, aren't you? Safe from the media?'

'But at what price?' She stepped close, eyes flaring wide as if she felt it too, the simmer of charged awareness, palpable as a caress against overheated flesh. 'There are strings attached to this deal, aren't there? A price I have to pay?'

Domenico looked down his nose with all the hauteur six centuries of aristocratic breeding could provide. No one doubted his honour. Ever.

'I'm a man of my word.' He let that sink in. 'I offered you sanctuary and you have it. There are no strings.'

Yet if she hadn't been so stressed yesterday she'd have made sure of that before agreeing to his offer.

Domenico muffled a sliver of guilt that he'd taken advantage of her vulnerability. The stakes were too high, the trouble she could cause too severe for him to have second thoughts.

Her perfectly arched eyebrows rose. 'I'm free to leave?'

Domenico stepped back and gestured to the boats moored in the bay. 'I will even provide the transport.'

He wished she'd take him up on the offer. Yes, he wanted more from her but instinct warned him to be rid of her. He didn't relish the discordant tumble of his reactions to her. There was nothing logical or ordered about them. She made him feel…things he thought long dead.

Her eyes bored into his, as if she sought the very heart of him. 'But you want me out of the limelight.'

'Of course.' He shrugged. 'But I'm not keeping you prisoner. There are laws in this country.'

Her breath hissed and she stiffened, reading his implication. That one of them at least was honest and law-abiding.

Her mouth tightened but otherwise her face was blank. So much for vulnerability. Lucy Knight was as tough as nails.

'If you're staying…' He looked at her expectantly but she said nothing. 'We can discuss business when you're dressed.' He glanced at his watch. Eleven o'clock. 'Shall we say midday?'

'Why delay? I'd rather know what you want now.'

She spoke as if he hid something painful from her. He almost laughed at the idea. Once he made his offer she'd be eager enough.

'You're hardly dressed for business.'

She stuck her hands on her hips, her pose challenging and provocative. 'You'd be more comfortable if I wore a suit? Why can't you tell me now?'

Again those delicate eyebrows rose, as if she silently laughed at him.

Something snapped inside.

He stalked across till he stood close enough to inhale the scent of soap and fragrant female flesh. Close enough to hook an arm round her and haul her flush against him if he chose. Instead he kept his hands clenched at his sides.

She refused to shift. Even though she had to tip her head back to look at him, exposing her slim throat. Heat twisted in his belly, part unwilling admiration at her nerve, part implacable fury.

His gaze held hers as his pulse thumped once, twice, three times. The artery at her throat flickered rapidly and she swallowed. Yet she didn't look away.

Charged seconds ticked by. Her pupils dilated. His senses stirred. Did he imagine that hint of musky arousal in his nostrils? The quiver of anticipation in the air?

Her breasts rose with her rapid breathing, almost but not quite brushing against him. The woman staring back defiantly was no modest, unprotected innocent.

The thought pulled him up. He'd almost forgotten this was about her, not him.

She wasn't as unaffected as she pretended. He

saw the fine tremor running under her skin. Her tongue flicked out to swipe her lips and he bit back a smile. For it wasn't a consciously slow, seductive movement but sure evidence her mouth had dried. Nerves or arousal?

Domenico leaned close, letting the heat of her body drench him. Her lashes flickered and her trembling pulse accelerated. His quickened too.

Holding her gaze, he reached out and snagged her belt. Instantly she stiffened, but she didn't retreat.

Was that a challenge in her eyes?

Her breath was a warm, sweet sigh against his chin as he tugged the bow undone, loosening the fabric around her.

Domenico bent his head and her pursed lips softened. Her eyes widened and something flickered there. Fear or anticipation?

'My office in an hour. You'll be less easily distracted if you're fully dressed.'

He straightened, spun on his heel and left her.

Lucy's breath came in great gulps. Her heart pumped so hard she thought it might jump out of her ribcage.

Domenico Volpe strolled back to the villa with an easy, loose-limbed grace that made her want to hurl something at his broad back. In dark trousers and an open-necked shirt he was the picture of elegant ease. He looked casual, sexy, utterly unaffected by the charge of erotic energy that hammered through her.

She shivered despite the molten heat inside. Her nipples were tight buds of need and she was wet between the legs. Because of the way he'd *looked* at her. Just looked!

How was that possible?

She shook her head, torn between shock, fury and shame. Her body betrayed her. *And he knew it.*

She'd read triumph in his eyes when he'd undone her belt. Had he sensed the voluptuous shiver she couldn't suppress? The tension in her body that had as much to do with fighting her traitorous desire as standing up to him?

With fumbling hands she pulled the wrap tight, as if it made any difference now. He didn't even look back. He was so confident he'd made his point.

That she was vulnerable to him. That she…desired him.

The realisation blasted Lucy's ragged confidence. She wanted to pretend it wasn't true. But hiding would get her nowhere. She had to face it.

Yet surely the fledgling attraction she'd once felt for him was dead, crushed by his cruel assumption of her guilt. She assured herself this wasn't about

Domenico Volpe. It was what he represented—hot
animal sex. Despite his shuttered gaze and his in-
sultingly casual contempt, there was no mistaking
the virile male beneath the expensive clothes.

Who wouldn't be affected by such a potently masculine man?

Lucy had been celibate so long, so cut off from
attractive men. This was her body's way of reminding her she was female, that was all.

She shoved aside the fact that she'd felt nothing
like this around Chiara's Uncle Rocco.

Maybe her distrust of Domenico Volpe, the fact
that her emotions were engaged because of the past,
gave a piquancy to her response.

Whatever it was, she had no intention of suc-
cumbing to weakness. As he'd soon learn.

He was seated at an enormous desk when she entered his study. Of course he'd take the position of
power. Lucy had dealt with enough officials to recognise the tactic.

He was like the rest. Predictable.

He turned from the computer to survey her,
taking in her denim skirt and the blue shirt that
matched her eyes. It was the nicest one she owned
and had always made her feel confident. Now it was

233

years out of date and a snug fit around the bust but it was the best she could do.

His appraising glance told her he wasn't impressed. Or was he recalling her standing, spellbound, as she let him undo her robe? The idea stiffened her resolve and she crossed the room, leaving the door open.

'You had business to discuss?' She sat in the chair before his desk and crossed her legs in a show of nonchalance.

He seemed riveted to the movement and she suppressed a surge of satisfaction. So, he wasn't as remote as he appeared. The knowledge gave her a sliver of hope.

'Yes.' He cleared his throat. 'I have a proposition for you.'

'Really? I'd have thought I was the last woman you'd ever proposition, Signor Volpe.'

His gaze darted to her face and she read simmering anger there. She could deal with anger. She clung to her own like a lifeline. It was preferable to the other feelings he evoked.

'Do tell,' she purred. 'I'm all ears.'

She had to bite back a smile when a frown furrowed his brow. She liked the fact that she pricked his self-possession. It wasn't fair that even scowling he still looked lethally gorgeous. Not that she cared.

'You want privacy and peace from the press. I want you out of the limelight. Our interests coincide.'

'So?'

'So I'd like to make the situation permanent.'

It was Lucy's turn to frown. 'I don't understand.'

He pushed a typed document towards her. 'Read that and you will. I've had it drawn up in English.'

'How considerate.' Perhaps he thought her Italian, learned behind bars, was inadequate. He had no idea the hours she'd spent poring over Italian legal documents.

She slid the paper towards her. It was a contract. She turned the page, heart racing as she read what he planned. She could barely believe it.

Finally she sat back. 'You really are desperate to keep me quiet.'

His dark eyes gleamed. 'Hardly desperate.'

'No? A lot of people would be fascinated to know how much you're offering to stop me talking.'

His look turned baleful. His voice when it came was a lethal whisper scudding through the silence. 'Is that a threat?'

'No threat, Signor Volpe. An observation.'

His eyes pinioned her and her breathing grew shallow. But she refused to be intimidated.

'I want peace for my family.' Yet his eyes didn't

plead, they demanded. 'You can't say the offer isn't generous.'

'Generous?' The money on the table was stupefying. Enough to fund that new start in life she'd longed for. Enough to establish herself immediately, even though what was left of her family rejected her. Looked at that way, it was tempting.

'On condition that I don't talk about your brother, his wife, their son, their household, you or anyone associated with your family or the court case.' She ticked the list off on her fingers. 'Nor could I discuss my time in jail or the legal proceedings.'

Indignation settled like a burning ember, firing her blood. 'I'd be gagged from making any comment, ever.'

'You have to earn the money I'm offering.' He shrugged those powerful shoulders, leaning back behind the massive desk, symbol of the power he wielded.

'Earn!' Lucy was sick of being the one ground down by those in authority. The one forced to carry the blame.

Searing anger sparked from that slow burning ember in her belly. She pushed the document across the desk.

'No.'

'Pardon?'

Lucy loved his perplexed expression. How many people said no to this man? She bet precious few women ever had.

'I'm not interested.'

'You've got to be joking. You need money.'

'How do you know that?' She leaned forward. 'Don't tell me you managed to access my private bank details.' She shook her head. 'That would be a criminal offence.'

His teeth bared in a grimace that told her he fought to retain his temper. Good. Goading him was the closest she'd get to revenge and she was human enough to revel in it.

'If you expect a better offer you'll have a long wait. My price is fair.'

'Fair?' Her voice rose. 'No price is *fair* if I can't tell my side of the story. You really expect me to forget what happened to me?' Disbelief almost choked her. 'If I took your blood money it would be tantamount to admitting guilt.' The thought made her sick to the stomach.

'And so?'

'Damn you, Domenico Volpe!' Lucy shot from her chair and skewered him with a glare that should have shrivelled him to ashes in his precious executive chair. 'I refuse to soothe your conscience or that of your sister-in-law.'

He rose and leaned across so his face was a breath away from hers.

'What are you implying?'

'Don't play the innocent.' She braced her hands on the table, firing the words at him. 'Your family's influence was what convicted me.'

'You have the temerity to hint the trial wasn't fair? Because of us?'

She had to give him credit. He looked so furious he'd have convinced anyone. Except someone who'd been behind bars for years because of his precious family.

'Come *on*! What chance did I stand with an overworked public defender against your power and influence?'

'The evidence pointed overwhelmingly to you.'

'But it wasn't true.' Her breath came in uneven pants as she faced him across the desk.

'You'd be well advised to sign.' His look sent a tremor of fear racing through her.

But he couldn't hurt her. Not now. She was free. She had no one and almost no money, but she had integrity. He couldn't take that.

'Now who's making threats?' She stared into eyes that glowed like molten steel.

Deliberately she leaned across his desk, her lips almost grazing his cheek, her nostrils filling with the heady spice scent of him. His eyes widened in shock and she wondered if she'd looked like that out in the garden when he'd come close enough to kiss her.

'I don't respond to threats,' she breathed in a whisper that caressed his scrupulously shaved jaw. 'The answer is still no.'

CHAPTER FIVE

DAMN THE WOMAN.

Domenico paced his study, furious he hadn't broken the deadlock. Lucy Knight still rejected his offer.

It stuck in his craw to give her anything but it was the only way to stop her selling her story. Then what privacy would Pia and Taddeo have? The scandal could go on for years, dogging Taddeo as he grew.

Money was the obvious lever to get what he needed. She was desperate for cash. If she'd had funds she'd have spent it on a top-flight defence team.

A splinter of discomfort pierced him, remembering her inexperienced, under-prepared lawyer. Watching his ineffectual efforts had made Domenico actually consider intervening to organise a more capable defender.

To defend the woman who'd killed Sandro!

Perhaps if he hadn't known she was guilty he

would have. But how could he doubt the over-whelming evidence against her?

A mere week before Sandro's death Lucy Knight had bumped into Domenico, literally, at an exhibition of baroque jewellery. He was supervising the inclusion of some family pieces but had been distracted, outrageously so, by the charms of the delightful young Englishwoman who'd blushed and stammered so prettily. She'd looked at the gems with unfeigned delight and at him with something like awe.

Yet it was her hesitation to accept his spur of the moment invitation to coffee that had hooked him. How long since a woman had even pretended to resist him?

Coffee had turned into a stroll through the Forum, lunch at a tucked away trattoria and an afternoon sightseeing. He'd enjoyed himself more than he could remember with a woman who was just Lucy to his Domenico. A woman whose eyes sparkled with unconcealed awareness, yet who trembled with innocent hesitation when he merely took her hand. She was smart, fun and refreshingly honest. Enough to make him believe he'd found someone special and rare.

She'd evoked a slew of emotions. Passion, delight and a surprising protectiveness that had kept him from sweeping her off to his bed then and there. For the connection between them had been sizzling, each touch electric.

She'd been different from every other woman, her impact so profound he'd suggested meeting again when he returned to Rome.

In New York he'd counted the hours to his return.

Till he'd seen Lucy in a news report, doused in his brother's blood as she was led away by the police.

His heart stuttered at the memory.

Then piece by piece he'd heard from Pia and Sandro's staff the truth about Lucy. How she'd seduced his brother and flaunted her power over him.

She must have known who Domenico was at the gallery and engineered the meeting. Why stick with Sandro, whose wife was already making a fuss about his affair, when his brother—just as rich and single to boot—was available? *And just as susceptible.*

Domenico thrust a hand through his hair. He'd fallen for her with an ease that shamed and angered him.

No. She'd brought on the result of the trial herself.

Yet he couldn't douse his awareness of her. The delicacy of her features snagged his attention again and again, as did the proud, wilful angle of her jaw that appealed even as it repelled.

All afternoon he'd watched her. She appeared fascinated by the grounds, apparently content with the tranquillity here. Which made him wonder what her life had been like behind bars that she should revel in solitude.

There it was again. This unholy interest in the woman. She should mean nothing to him but a problem to be solved. Instead he found himself... intrigued.

And that tiny dead of night niggle was back, disturbing his rest.

He strode to the window, hands jammed in his pockets.

She gave him no peace. There she was at the end of the garden. The afternoon sun burnished her hair, making it glint like gold as she tipped her head back. Her obvious sensual delight was far too alluring, the way she held her arms open to embrace the heat, her deep breaths that drew his eyes to her delectable breasts.

She stiffened, head turning and arms folding in a classic defensive pose. Her tension was obvious as a figure approached from the villa. Rocco, his Head of Security.

Rocco held out a broad-brimmed hat. For a moment she stood stiff, as if unwilling to accept it. Then Rocco spoke and her defensive posture eased.

She took the hat and put it on. Rocco spoke again and she shook her head. Was that laughter he caught in the distance?

Domenico stared, fascinated. Lucy Knight was so wary, stiffening the instant he or his security staff came near. To see her relaxed and laughing… Why? Because Rocco had offered her protection from the sun? It was a simple consideration any-one would offer.

Yet look how she responded. Now they were in conversation. She must be asking about landmarks for he pointed to the mainland and she nodded, leaning close.

Domenico frowned, not liking the swirl of dis-content that rose as he watched them together.

The difference in her was remarkable. Domenico recalled the way her face had lit up at lunch when the maid served a delicious tiramisu, saying it was the cook's speciality, prepared to welcome the new guest. Lucy's eyes had widened then softened with appreciation and shock before she realised he was watching and looked away. Later she'd made a point of telling the maid how much she'd enjoyed the dessert.

The tiramisu was a little thing, a familiar cour-tesy to a guest, yet Lucy Knight had responded with surprised delight.

Was she so unused to consideration or kindness?

Given how she'd lived for the past several years it wasn't surprising.

What had she said when she'd rejected his offer out of hand? That she didn't respond to threats?

Domenico's brain snapped into gear. He'd seen her proud defiance, her cool calm and her haughty, almost self-destructive need to assert her independence. Look at the way she'd faced the paparazzi.

If the threats didn't work…what *would* she respond to?

Perhaps there was another way to get what he needed.

Instead of demands, persuasion might be more effective. Didn't they say you could catch more flies with honey than vinegar?

Lucy shut her eyes and listened to the drowsy hum of bees in the garden and, below, the soft shush of waves. She was so incredibly lethargic, mind and body reacting as if, for the first time in years, she didn't need to be constantly on guard. It was easy to relax here, too easy, given she had a future to organise and decisions to make. She should—

'I thought I'd find you here.' The deep voice swirled across her nerve ends, jerking them into tingling life.

She sat up abruptly in the low sun lounger. Standing between her and the sun was her host. For a moment she saw only an imposing silhouette, rampantly male with those broad shoulders, long legs and classically sculpted head. Her heart quickened with something other than surprise.

She scrambled to rise.

'Don't move.' He put his hand out to stop her and sank onto a nearby seat.

She subsided, then gathered herself. Obviously he was here to demand she sign his contract. So much for the peace he'd promised!

She sat straight, knees together, watching suspiciously.

'I thought I'd take you on a tour of the grounds.'

Lucy stared at him, but he returned her disbelieving look blandly.

'Why?'

His black brows arched infinitesimally and ridiculously she felt a sliver of jab at her brusqueness. As if she cared what he thought of her manners. Once upon a time she'd have bantered polite words but not now. He'd forfeited her trust.

'If you're going to stay you should learn the lie of the land.'

He sounded so reasonable. So civilised.

But then he was a civilised man. Look at the way

he'd invited her to sit at his table today, as if she was a guest, not the enemy. She'd seen the tension in him, had felt its echo in her own discomfort, but if he was able to bear her company she refused to let him know how confused and edgy she was in his.

'You don't want to spend time with me.' The words grated from her tight throat. 'Why suggest it?' The words sounded churlish, but it was the truth.

She waited for his annoyance to show, but his face remained impassive. What was he thinking?

'You're a guest in my villa and—'

'Hardly.' Her fingers curved around the edge of her seat. 'More a burden.'

'I invited you here.' He paused as if expecting her to interrupt. 'As your host I have an obligation. I need to ensure your safety.'

'Safety?' Incredulous, she surveyed the delightful garden. 'Don't tell me, you have meat-eating killer ants that prey on people who fall asleep on the lawn?'

Was that a smile she saw, quickly suppressed? The fleeting hint of a dimple in that lean cheek was ridiculously attractive. Her response to it scared her. 'Or rabid guard dogs who can sniff out an ex-convict if they stray near anything precious?'

No smile now with that blatant reminder of reality. Lucy told herself she preferred it that way. The last thing she needed was to find the man appealing again.

'No animal dangers but there are things you need to be wary of, including an old well and some sink holes.' He paused, obviously waiting for her assent.

What could she say? His offer sounded reasonable, though the chances of her falling down a hole were nil.

He wanted something. Why else seek her out?

To badger her into signing his contract? She was strong enough to withstand threats.

Besides, she was curious. She hated to admit it but it still felt as if there was unfinished business between them. Surely a little time in his company would erase that unsettling notion? Then she could leave without that niggle at her consciousness. It would be a relief to banish him from her thoughts.

'If you think it necessary, by all means show me the dangers of your island.'

'Va bene.' He stood and extended a hand.

Lucy pretended not to notice. The last thing she needed was physical contact with a man whose presence threw her senses into overdrive.

She stood quickly, brushing down her skirt.

'The first thing you must remember is to wear a hat at all times.'

'Like you do?' She stared pointedly at his dark hair, bare to the blazing sun.

Again that hint of a dimple marked his cheek, playing havoc with her insides. Lucy drew herself up, quenching the memory of how his smile had once made her heart skip and her mind turn to mush.

Clearly she'd been a passing amusement. Had he laughed at her gaucheness and wide-eyed wonder at Rome? And at being escorted by a stranger so handsome and attentive he'd all but made her swoon?

'I'm used to southern summers and I've got the skin for it.' He was right. His olive skin was burnished a deep bronze that enhanced the decisive contours of his face. 'Whereas you—'

'Have been behind bars.' Her chin jutted.

He shook his head slowly. 'You shouldn't finish other people's sentences. I was going to say you have a rare complexion. Cream and roses.' He leaned closer. 'And quite flawless.'

His eyes roved her face so thoroughly she felt his regard like the graze of a hand, making her flesh tingle. Her breath quickened and something unfamiliar spiralled deep inside, like the swoop and dip of swallows on the wing.

'Your English is good but the phrase is peaches and cream.' As if she believed he meant it! Prison pallor was more like. She looked away, needing to break the curious stillness that encompassed them.

'I say what I mean.' His voice was a low rumble from far too close. He raised his hand as if to touch her, and then let it drop. 'Your skin has the lustre of new cream, or of pearls, with just a hint of rose.'

Lucy swung round to face him fully, hands on hips as she leaned forward to accuse him of making fun at her expense. She was no longer a gullible young thing to be taken in by smooth talk.

But the look on his face stole the harsh response from her lips.

It stole her breath too.

There was no laughter in his expression. He looked stunned, as if shocked at his own words.

Burnished pewter eyes met hers, making her blood pound.

Something arced between them, something like static electricity that drew the hairs at her nape erect and dried her mouth.

Abruptly they moved apart.

She wasn't the woman he'd thought he knew.

Domenico watched her navigate the dusty path at the far end of the island with alacrity, as if exploring a semi-wilderness was high on her list of things to do. Her head swung from side to side as

she took in the spectacular views and the country-
side he always found so restful.

What had happened to the girl who thrived on
bright lights and male attention? Who hankered
after expensive jewellery and the excitement of a
cosmopolitan city filled with boutiques, nightclubs,
bars and men?

Was she hiding her boredom? She did a good job.

She'd even forgotten to scowl at him and her face
had lost that shuttered look in the last half hour. Relaxed, she looked younger, softer.

Dangerously attractive.

There was a vibrancy about her he hadn't seen
since the day they'd met.

Perhaps she'd been seduced by the warmth of the
afternoon and the utter peace of the place. She'd
changed. The tension radiating from her like a
shield was gone.

She paused, eyes on a butterfly floating past, as
if its simple beauty fascinated her.

As she fascinated him.

The realisation dropped into his thoughts like a
stone plummeting into a calm millpond.

How could it be? He carried Sandro's memory
strong within him. Any interest in her should be
impossible.

Yet why had he chosen to oversee her stay here?

It wasn't necessary. A lawyer could witness her signing the contract.

The truth was Domenico was here because something about Lucy Knight made him curious even now. Something he couldn't put his finger on. Something he needed to understand before she walked out of his life for ever.

'Is that a ruined *castle*?' The husky thread of pleasure in her voice brought Domenico back to the present.

'It is.'

'Yet you built your villa on the opposite end of the island.'

He shrugged. 'The aspect is better there. This was built to defend, not enjoy.'

'Strange,' she mused as they stopped to take in the scene. 'I had pegged you as someone who'd rather rebuild the old family estate than start afresh. After all, you live in the family palazzo in Rome.'

She shifted abruptly and he had the impression she wished she hadn't spoken. The palazzo conjured memories of what lay between them.

'You think I'm bound by tradition?'

She lifted her shoulders. 'I have no idea. I don't know you.'

That was the problem, Lucy decided. She'd thought she knew Domenico Volpe. All those weeks during the trial he'd been like an avenging angel, stonily silent and chillingly furious, waiting for her to be convicted. His eyes, cold as snow yet laser-hot when they rested on her, had told her all she needed to know about him.

Yet now she found him approachable—courteous and civilised. As if his lethal anger had never existed. She caught glimpses of the man she'd been wildly attracted to all those years ago. The man who'd made such an impression that in her innocence she'd thought she'd found The One.

Lucy stole a look as he stared at the tumbled stones. His severe features held a charisma that threatened to steal her breath. Abruptly she looked away, hating her quickened pulse.

'Because I honour family tradition doesn't mean I live in the past.'

He lounged against a stone wall beyond which was a deep ravine. A moat, she supposed, staring at the castle beyond. But though she kept her eyes on the view, she was supremely aware of her companion. In faded denim jeans that clung to powerful thighs and a dark short-sleeved shirt that revealed the sinewy strength of his tanned forearms, he looked far too real. Too earthy and sexy. She'd never seen him like this.

Lucy told herself a change of clothes meant nothing. Yet she couldn't suppress the idea that she was closer to the real Domenico Volpe than in his city mansion.

She shied from asking herself why she wanted to know him at all.

Lucy shrugged. 'I thought you'd prefer the castle.'

'To lord it over my subjects?'

She shook her head. This man didn't need external proof of his authority. It was all there—stamped in the austere beauty of his face. He'd been born to wealth but he'd grown into a man used to command.

'Since family tradition means so much, you could restore the place.'

'Ah, but this is an acquisition, not an inheritance. I bought it years ago to celebrate my first success.'

Lucy turned to meet his gaze. 'Success?'

'*Si*.' His brows rose and she caught a flash of steel in his eyes. 'Or did you think we Volpes have no need of work? That we sit on our inherited wealth and do nothing?' His tone bit.

Once she'd have thought that was precisely what his family did, after seeing the ultra-luxurious way his brother and sister-in-law lived. Pia had never lifted a finger to do anything for herself, or her child.

Instantly guilt flared, twisting Lucy's stomach.

Pia might have been completely spoiled but her lack of involvement with little Taddeo had stemmed from her inability to bond with the baby. Lucy knew how much guilt and shame, not to mention fear that had caused the poor woman. No wonder she'd been insecure.

'I see that's exactly what you think.'

'Sorry?' Lucy blinked and turned, surprised to find herself so close to the man who now loomed over her.

'You view us as lazy parasites, perhaps?' His voice was low and amused but Lucy knew in her bones that amusement hid anger.

'Not at all.' She tilted her chin to meet his stare unflinchingly. 'I know your wealth began with your inheritance but you struck out on your own as an entrepreneur, risking your capital on projects others wouldn't touch. Your flair for managing risk made you the golden-haired boy of the European business world when other ventures were collapsing around you. You have a reputation for hard work and phenomenal luck.'

'It's not luck,' he murmured. 'It's careful calculation.'

Lucy shrugged. 'Whatever the reason, the markets call you *Il Volpe*, the fox, for good reason.'

'Fascinating that you should know so much about

me.' His voice brushed across her skin like the touch of rich velvet. A ripple of pleasure followed it.

Instinctively Lucy made to step back, then stopped.

Never back down. Never retreat. Weakness shown was an invitation to be walked over.

'It seemed prudent to know what I was up against.'

His eyebrows soared. '*We* weren't in conflict.'

'No?' She shook her head. 'Your family's influence put me behind bars.'

His eyes narrowed to deadly slits. Heat sizzled at the look he gave her.

'Let's get this straight. My family did no more than wait the outcome of the trial.'

Lucy opened her mouth to protest but his raised hand stopped her.

'No! You imply *what*? That we rigged the trial? That we bribed the police or judiciary?' He shook his head in a fine show of anger. 'The evidence convicted you, Ms Knight. Nothing else.' He paused and she watched him grapple for control, his strong features taut, his muscles bunched.

He drew a deep breath and Lucy saw his wide chest expand. When he spoke his voice was crisp. 'You have my word as a Volpe on it. We live within the law.'

There was no mistaking his emotion. It was almost convincing.

'You don't believe me?' His eyes narrowed.

In truth she didn't know. There was no doubt she'd been disadvantaged by the quality of her legal team compared with the ruthless efficiency and dogged determination of the prosecution. And it was obvious that sympathy lay with Pia, the beautiful grieving widow and young mother. Lucy knew that sympathy had given Pia's evidence more weight than it deserved. At Lucy's expense.

Plus Bruno Scarlatti, Sandro's bodyguard and the prosecution's chief witness, was ex-police. He'd shone in court. His evidence had been clear and precise, unclouded by emotion. That evidence had damned her and swayed the court. She was sure his ex-police status had weighed with the investigators too, though she had no proof.

'I…don't know.' For the first time confusion filled her, not the righteous indignation that had burned so long.

'I'm not used to having my word doubted.' Hauteur laced Domenico's tone.

Lucy's lips curled in a sour half smile. 'Believe me, it doesn't get any easier with time.'

His eyes widened as he realised she was talking

about herself. She almost laughed, but there was nothing funny about it.

Even after all this time, bearing the burden of public guilt was like carrying an open wound. She wondered if she'd ever feel whole again while she carried that lie with her. It had changed her life irrevocably.

Now the dreams she'd cherished about starting afresh seemed just that—dreams. How could they not, with Sylvia's cruel betrayal and the eager press waiting to scoop more stories? How would she find the peace she craved to build a new life?

She turned away, her joy in the place forgotten.

'Wait.' The word stabbed the silence.

'What?' Reluctantly she faced him.

'This—' his hand slashed between them '—isn't helpful.'

'So?'

'So—' his nostrils flared as he breathed deep '—I propose a truce. You're my guest. I'll treat you as such and you'll reciprocate. No more accusations, by either of us.'

Was this to soften her up so she'd sign his paper? Or was it, a little squiggle of hope tickled her, because he had doubts about her guilt?

No. That hope died as it was born. He'd shown no doubt in court. Not once. He'd spurned her as if she were unclean. He didn't want to absolve her, just strike an accord that would give them peace while they shared the villa.

Peace. That was what she craved, wasn't it?

'Agreed.' Lucy put her hand out and, after a surprised glance, he took it.

She regretted it as soon as his fingers enveloped hers. Fire sparked and spread from his touch, running tendrils of heat along her arm to her cheeks, breasts and belly. Even down her legs, where her knees locked against sudden weakness.

She sucked in a shocked breath at the intensity of that physical awareness.

Did he feel it? His eyes gleamed deep silver and his sculpted lips tightened.

His next words were the last she expected to hear.

'So you will call me Domenico, *si*? And I'll call you Lucy.'

Time warped. It was as if they were back in Rome, chance met strangers, her heart thundering as their eyes locked for the first time.

His gaze bored into hers, challenging her to admit the idea of his name on her lips discomfited her. Or was it the sound of her own name, like a tantalising caress in his rich, deep voice, that made her pulse falter?

'I don't think—'

'To seal our truce,' he insisted, his gaze intent as if reading the thrill of shock snaking through her.

'Of course.' She refused to let him fluster her, especially over something so trivial.

Yet it didn't feel trivial. It felt... Lucy groped for a word to describe the sensations assailing her but failed.

With a nod he released her and stepped away. Yet Lucy still felt the imprint of his hand on hers and her spine tingled at the memory of him saying her name with that delicious hint of an accent.

She had the uncomfortable feeling she'd just made a huge mistake.

CHAPTER SIX

THEY WERE SILENT as they walked along the beach to the villa. Late afternoon light lengthened their shadows and for the first time in weeks Domenico felt something like peace, listening to the rhythm of the sea and their matched steps.

Peace, with Lucy Knight beside him!

His business negotiations had reached a crucial phase that would normally have consumed every waking hour. On top of that was Pia's near hysterical response to the latest press reports, and his own turbulent reactions to the release of his brother's killer.

And here he was walking with her in the place that was his refuge from the constant demands on his time. Was he mad letting her in here?

Yet the stakes were too high. He had to convince her—

Beside him she stopped. He turned, wondering what had caught her attention.

In the peachy light her hair was a nimbus of gold,

backlit by the sun that lovingly silhouetted her shape. She'd taken off her sandals and stood ankle-deep in the froth of gentle waves. She looked...appealing.

His pulse thudded and he realised she was watching him. Her gaze branded his skin.

Instinctively he moved closer, needing to read her expression. What he saw made premonition jitter through him. Was she going to agree to his terms? He schooled his face, knowing better than to rush her.

'Lucy?' Her name tasted good on his tongue. Too good. This was business. Business and the protection of his family. It was his duty to protect Taddeo and Pia now Sandro wasn't here to do it. The thought of Sandro renewed his resolve.

'I...' Her gaze skated away and he leaned in, willing her to continue. She drew a deep breath, straining her blouse across ripe breasts. Domenico berated himself for noticing, but he noticed everything about her. Was that an asset or a penalty?

'You?' Expectation buzzed. It wasn't like her to hesitate. She was aggressively forthright.

Her eyes met his and something punched deep in his belly. Gone were her defiance and her anger. Instead he read something altogether softer in her face.

'I never told you.' She paused and bit her lip, reminding him in a flash of blinding memory of the girl he'd met all those years ago. The one whose forget-me-not eyes had haunted him with their apparent shock and bewildered innocence. Who'd been a conundrum with her mix of uncertainty and belligerent, caustic defiance.

His belly tightened. There was no logic to the fact she unsettled him as no other woman had.

'Sorry. I'm usually more coherent.'

'You can say that again.'

Her lips twisted. Then she straightened, her jaw tensing as she met his eyes head-on.

'We agreed not to make accusations and I understand there's no point protesting my innocence.' She inhaled through flared nostrils. 'But there's something you need to hear.' She paused as if expecting him to cut her off, but Domenico had no intention of interrupting.

'I'm sorry about your brother.' Her gaze didn't waver and Domenico felt the force of her words as a palpable weight. 'His death was a tragedy for his wife and child, for *all* his family. He was a good man, a caring one.' She released a breath that shivered on the air between them. 'I'm sorry he died and I'm sorry I was involved.'

Stunned, Domenico watched her lips form the words.

After all this time…

He'd never expected an apology, though he'd told himself an admission of guilt would salve the pain of Sandro's loss.

She didn't confess, yet, to Domenico's amazement, her words of regret struck a chord deep inside. He stared at her and she didn't try to hide, even lifted her face as if to open herself to his scrutiny.

For the first time he felt the barriers drop between them and he knew for this moment truth hovered. Truth and honest regret.

'Thank you.' His voice was hoarse from grief that seemed fresh as ever. But with the pain came something like peace.

The cynic in him stood ready to accuse her of an easy lie, a sop to his anger. Yet what he saw in Lucy's face drowned the voice of cynicism. 'I appreciate it.'

Her lips twisted in a crooked smile. 'I'm glad.' She paused then severed eye contact, turning towards the sea. 'I wrote to your sister-in-law some time ago, saying the same thing. I'm not sure she even read the letter.'

'You wrote to Pia?' It was the first he'd heard of it

and usually Pia was only too ready to lean on him for emotional support.

He stared at the woman he'd thought he understood. How well did he know her after all? She confounded his certainties time and again.

She made him feel so many unexpected emotions.

A day later Domenico stood at his study window, drawn from his computer by the sound of laughter.

On the paved area by the head of the stairs to the beach were Rocco's niece, Chiara, and Lucy, neat in her denim skirt and blouse. Lucy bent to mark the flagstones in a square chalk pattern and Domenico fought to drag his eyes from the denim tight around her firm backside.

Heat flared as his gaze roved her ripe curves.

Too often he found himself watching Lucy with distinctly male appreciation.

He switched his gaze to Chiara as, shaking her head, she took the chalk and drew her own patterns, circular this time. As she finished, understanding dawned. They were playing a children's game: Mondo. Watching Chiara gesticulate he guessed she was explaining her game rather than the English Hopscotch, that Lucy had marked.

'You wanted me, boss?' Rocco tapped at the door.

Did he? Domenico couldn't recall. Frustration

bit. He'd been distracted all morning. Lucy and her refusal to sign his contract undermined his focus.

'Have you seen who your niece is playing with?' His voice grated as he realised it wasn't Lucy's obstinacy that distracted him. It was the woman herself—prickly, proud and, he hated to admit it, intriguing in ways that had nothing to do with the danger she posed to his family.

'They're good together, aren't they?'

Domenico frowned. 'You have no qualms about Chiara playing with a woman who served time for killing a man?'

Not just any man. His brother. Domenico's breath was harsh in his constricted lungs.

There was a long silence. He turned to find Rocco regarding him steadily. 'The past is the past, boss. Even the court said it wasn't premeditated. Besides, she loves children. Anyone can see that.' He nodded to the garden and Domenico turned to see Lucy ushering Chiara, who'd grown boisterous with excitement, away from the steps.

Domenico felt a sliver of something like shame, seeing her concern for Chiara. Even the prosecution at her trial had acknowledged she'd been a reliable carer for little Taddeo.

'Mamma trusts her with Chiara. You can't say better.'

Rocco's *mamma* was a redoubtable woman, canny and an excellent judge of character. As housekeeper to the Volpes for over thirty years, she and Sandro between them had brought Domenico up when his parents had died.

'Maybe Signorina Knight isn't the woman you think.'

Domenico stiffened. He didn't need Rocco's advice, even if he was the best security manager he'd ever had.

Yet once lodged in his brain, his words couldn't be dismissed.

Was she the same woman he'd heard about all those years ago? Greedy, self-centred, luring his brother into indiscretion under his wife's nose? If he hadn't experienced first-hand the powerful tug of her innocent seductress routine he'd never have believed Sandro would be unfaithful.

She had been only eighteen then; had the last years changed her?

He saw glimpses of a far different woman. One with surprising depths—an inner core of strength and what he suspected was her own brand of integrity. One that reminded him a little of the golden girl who'd once snared his attention, but far, far tougher and sassy. Besides, that girl had been a mirage.

Frustration rose. He wasn't used to uncertainty, either in business or with women. Usually his instincts for both served him well.

Was he seeing what he wanted to see?

More important, did he see what *she* wanted him to see? Unfamiliar tension coiled in Domenico's belly. She'd got under his skin, inserting doubt where previously there'd been certainty.

Why maintain her innocence after all this time? Unbidden, he recalled again her inexperienced legal representative. Would the trial's outcome have been different with a better lawyer?

A twinge of discomfort pierced him.

Domenico's mouth tightened. His curiosity had as much to do with attraction at a primal level as it did the need for understanding. This was about more than gagging Lucy Knight from spreading stories that would harm his family.

The stakes were far more personal.

Lucy was walking back to the villa when a figure loomed before her.

'How would you like to come snorkelling?'

Suspicion welled as she looked into Domenico's unreadable grey eyes. True, they'd agreed a truce. True, he let her have the run of the estate, even access to the Internet so she could trawl fruitlessly for jobs—as if anyone would take her on with her history. But taking her on an excursion?

Lucy shook her head. 'I should check my email.' As if there was a chance some employer had bothered to respond to the dozens of queries she'd sent. Given the poor economic climate, attracting an employer's interest would be a miracle. Even if she managed that, there were the hurdles of character and criminal record checks.

'You can do that when we return. Come on, it will be good to get off the island.'

'Why?'

What did he want? Remembering his glowering scowl when they'd first met, a fatal boating accident seemed possible. But lately… No, he wasn't a violent man, just one used to getting what he wanted. And he wanted her to sign his contract. Was he trying to soften her up?

He shrugged and to her chagrin she followed the movement of those wide, straight shoulders with a fascination she still couldn't conquer.

'Because I'm fed up with emails and performance indicators and financial statements. It's time for a break.' His lips curved in a one-sided smile that carved a long dimple in one cheek and snared her breath before it could reach her lungs.

The man was indecently attractive.

'I really should—'

'You're not avoiding me, are you, Lucy?'

Stoically she ignored the way his hint of an accent turned her ordinary name into something delicious. It had made her weak at the knees the day they'd met.

'Why would I do that?'

His eyes sizzled pure silver—the colour of a lightning bolt against a stormy sky. She could almost feel the ground shake beneath her feet from its impact.

Again he shrugged. This time she kept her eyes on his face. 'Perhaps I make you nervous.'

He was dead right. No matter how often she told herself Domenico had no power over her, instinct eclipsed logic and fear shivered through her. A fear that had nothing to do with his wealth and influence and everything to do with him as a potently attractive, fascinating man.

She'd washed her hands of him long ago. She'd seen him in court and her heart had leapt, believing he was there for her. Instead he'd cut her dead, so sure of her guilt before the trial even began. She'd been gutted.

Why did she still respond to him?

'Why should I be nervous?'

'I have no idea.' Yet his expression was knowing, as if he read her tension.

Did he guess the shockingly erotic fantasies that invaded her dreams each night? Fantasies that featured Domenico Volpe, not as disapproving and distant, but as her hot, earthily sexy lover? Lucy swallowed hard, reassuring herself that if he knew the last thing he'd do was invite her to spend time with him.

'I don't have a swimsuit.' Her voice emerged husky and she watched his attention shift to her mouth. Her lips tingled and heat bloomed deep in her belly.

He smiled. A fully fledged smile that made her heart skip a beat and alarm bells jangle.

'Be my guest. Find yourself a new one in the pool house.'

Lucy shook her head before she could be tempted. 'No, thank you.'

'Why not? Don't you want to go out there?' His gesture encompassed the azure shimmer of sea that had lured her since the moment she'd arrived.

How she'd love to do more than paddle in the shallows for once! She'd even toyed with the idea of a midnight skinny dip but it would be just her luck to be found by his security staff.

'I don't accept handouts.' She wasn't a charity case.

Domenico watched her for long seconds with a look that in anyone else she'd call astonished. When he spoke his voice had lost its teasing edge.

'It's not a handout. It's what we do for our guests. Rocco's *mamma* has a lovely time buying hats and wraps and swimsuits for guests. You'd be surprised how many people forget them on a seaside stay.'

Not like her. Lucy had been shuffled out of Rome in a hurry with no idea where she was heading. She wasn't like his other guests. She opened her mouth to say so when he spoke again.

'Come on, Lucy. Set your pride aside and enjoy yourself. I promise it won't make you obligated to me.'

That was what she hated, wasn't it? Feeling indebted to Domenico Volpe for this respite when she most needed it.

Of course he had his own agenda. He wanted to buy her silence.

Was she too proud? Self-sufficiency was something she'd learnt in a hard school. Did she take it too far?

The sound of the sea behind her and the tang of salt on the air reminded her that the only person to suffer for her pride was herself. Swimming in the Med was something she'd always wanted to do. When would she have the chance again? When she finally found a job she'd be too busy making ends meet to travel.

'Thank you,' she said at last. 'That would be… nice.'

Was that a flash of pleasure in Domenico's eyes? Not triumph as she'd half expected. Her brow puckered.

'Good.' He pointed her to the pool house. 'You'll find what you need up there. Don't forget a hat. I'll meet you at the boat.'

Fifteen minutes later Lucy hurried down the steps to the beach. She'd rifled through a treasure trove of designer swimwear, finally selecting the plainest one-piece she could find. No way was she flaunting herself before Domenico in a barely there string bikini. Nevertheless she felt strangely aware of the Lycra clinging to her body under her skirt and shirt. It reminded her of the flicker of heat she saw in his eyes, and her body's inevitable reaction—a softening deep inside.

So often she found him watching her, the hint of a frown on his wide forehead, as if she was some enigma he had to puzzle. Or was he calculating how long she'd hold out against the fortune he offered?

On condition she stopped proclaiming her innocence.

She set her jaw. The first thing she'd do when she found work was pay back the price of this swimsuit. Even if it took her months on the basic wage!

Lucy stepped into the boatshed, trying to calculate how much a designer swimsuit would set her back.

It was dim inside and it took a moment for her eyes to adjust. She blinked at the sleek outline of the speedboat moored inside. Was this the boat they were taking?

She turned, wondering if she should wait outside, when movement caught her eye.

On the far side of the boat a man came towards her—thickset with a bullish head and broad neck that spoke of blatant strength. He moved with surprising agility. His dark suit blended with the shadows but, as her eyes adjusted to the gloom, she caught the crooked line of a broken nose and hands the size of dinner plates.

The hair at her nape stood on end and terror engulfed her. She froze, recognition filling her.

The rusty taste of blood on her bitten tongue roused her. She drew a shuddering breath and catapulted towards the door. With every step she imagined one of those heavy hands grabbing her, capturing her, punishing her.

Lucy's breath sawed through constricted lungs

as she reached, hands outstretched, for the door. Her legs seemed to slow as if in a nightmare. She knocked over some tins that clattered to the floor and almost fell but kept going, eyes on the sunlit rectangle of freedom ahead, desperation driving her.

With a sob of fear she plunged outside, blinded by light, only to find her flight stopped by a hard, hot body.

He'd never held her but she knew it was Domenico. The scent of warm spice and pine, and something else, something so profound she had no name for it, told her it was him in the millisecond before his arms came round her, hugging her close.

'Please,' she gasped. 'Watch out! He's here. He's—'

She struggled to turn, but Domenico's grip was firm. She was plastered to him, her face pressed to his collarbone. One hand held her head against him and his other arm lashed protectively around her waist.

Lucy felt heat, strength and solidity. Safety. His heart beat steadily against her raised palm and, despite her fear relief weakened her knees. Tendrils of heat invaded her ice-numbed body, counteracting the horror that filled her.

'Lucy? What is it?' His deep voice ruffled her hair and wrapped itself around her.

She shook her head. 'Be careful! He—'

'I'm sorry, sir.' An unfamiliar voice came from behind her. 'I was putting provisions in the boat. I didn't mean to scare the lady.'

Lucy turned her head, eyes widening at the man who emerged from the boatshed.

He was a stranger.

Her heart leapt even as reaction set in and her knees buckled. She clung to Domenico. His grip tightened, holding her against him as if she belonged there.

Later she'd regret clinging to him, but now she was too overwhelmed by a sense of deliverance from danger.

It wasn't him.

The knowledge beat a rapid tattoo in her blood. She took in the worried face and bright eyes of the stranger. What she'd thought a bodyguard's suit was a casual uniform of dark trousers and shirt. The man was an employee, but not the one she'd feared. Even the crooked jut of his nose was different and his eyes held none of the gleaming malice she remembered.

In face of the stranger's concern Lucy tried to summon a reassuring smile but it wobbled too much.

'Lucy?' Domenico's broad palm rubbed her back

and comforting heat swirled from the point of contact. She pressed closer, arching into him.

'I'm sorry.' Her voice was husky. She turned as far as she could within Domenico's firm embrace. She should step free but couldn't dredge the strength to stand alone. 'I…overreacted. I saw someone coming towards me in the darkness and…'

'I'm sorry, *signorina*.' The big man looked solemn. 'I didn't mean—'

'No. Don't apologise.' Lucy's smile was more convincing now, though it felt like a rictus stretch of stiff muscles. 'It was my mistake.'

'It's okay, Salvo.' Domenico's deep voice was balm to shredded nerves. 'Everything's fine. You can leave us.'

With one last troubled look the man left and Lucy sagged. The rush of adrenalin was fading. She felt almost nauseous in the aftermath.

'Lucy? Come and sit in the shade.'

Suddenly, as if her brain had just engaged, she became fully conscious of how intimately they stood. The press of hard muscle and solid bone supporting her. The reassuring beat of his heart beneath her palm. The need to lean closer and lose herself in his embrace. The flare of pleasure at the differences between them—he was so utterly masculine against her melting weakness.

That realisation made her snap upright on a surge of horrified energy.

'I'm sorry.' Humiliation blurred her words as she struggled to remove herself from his hold. What must he think of her, clinging to him?

Bile churned her stomach. She knew what he must think. The prosecution at the trial had painted her as a femme fatale, using the promise of her body to win expensive favours from her indulgent boss. Domenico probably thought she was trying a similar tactic to win sympathy.

A shudder of self-loathing passed through her and she broke free. How could she have turned to him?

Her pace was uneven but she managed the few steps to the boatshed, putting her hand to its wall for support.

Stifling her shame and embarrassment, Lucy forced herself to turn. He stood, frowning, the line of his jaw razor-sharp and his grey eyes piercing.

'Now we're alone you can tell me who you thought you were running from. Who are you scared of?'

CHAPTER SEVEN

'SCARED?' LUCY GAVE a shaky laugh. Her hand dropped from the wall and she straightened. She swayed and Domenico discovered the heat curling through his belly had turned to anger.

It was a welcome change from the surge of hunger he'd known as she'd melted against him.

'Tell me, Lucy.' His tone was one his business associates obeyed without question.

Her chin jutted obstinately. 'There's nothing to tell. I saw someone coming towards me in the dark and panicked.'

Domenico shook his head. 'You don't panic.'

'How would you know? You're hardly an expert on me.'

But he was.

He'd spent the weeks of the trial trying to learn every nuance of her reactions—not that it had got him far. She'd been an enigma. But in the days since her release he'd been able to concentrate on little but her and he'd learned a lot. Enough to make him question his earlier, too easy assumptions.

ANNIE WEST 125

'You're no coward. You faced the paparazzi.' He added quietly, 'You faced *me*.'

Her eyes widened, acknowledgement if he'd needed it, of just how hard she'd found the last several days.

He remembered her hunched on the floor in the palazzo, her hand splayed where Sandro had breathed his last. Her blind pain had been almost unbearable to witness. What strength of character had it taken to face the place? The same strength it took to face him with an air of proud independence despite the tremors racking her.

Something hard and unforgiving inside him eased. Something that had already cracked when she'd expressed regret for Sandro's death. When he'd seen her playing with little Chiara. When he'd held her close and been torn between protective-ness and an utterly selfish desire for her soft, boun-tifully feminine body.

'There's nothing to tell.' But her eyes were clouded and her mouth white-rimmed. Her tension reignited the protectiveness that had enveloped him as he held her and felt the waves of fear shudder through her.

'Liar.'

She flinched, her face tightening.

'I thought we'd agreed to leave the accusations

behind.' There was desperate hauteur to her expression but she couldn't mask her pain.

'I'm not talking about the past. I'm talking about now. Here.' His slashing hand encompassed the scene that had just played out. 'You were scared out of your wits.'

Her pale eyebrows rose. 'Nothing scares me. After the last few years I'm unshockable.'

Looking into her unblinking gaze he almost believed her. Yet her desperate panting breath against his throat, the clutch of her hands and the feel of her body's response to overwhelming fear had been unmistakable.

Domenico stepped close and she stiffened. He kept going till he stood a breath away. Her face tilted up to his as he'd known it would. Lucy had proven time and again that she was no coward. She faced what she feared.

Until today. In the darkness of the boatshed.

His heart beat an uneven rhythm as he realised only true terror would have made this woman run.

'Who is he, Lucy?' He lifted a hand to her jaw, stroking his thumb over her silken flesh, feeling the jittering pulse. 'Who are you afraid of?'

Her eyelids flickered. She pressed into his touch and pleasure swirled deep inside.

'Bruno.' The word was a whisper. 'Bruno Scarlatti. Your brother's Head of Security.'

Domenico read her fear and knew she spoke the truth. He wanted to assure her she was safe. He wanted to tug her close and not let her go.

Because she was scared?

Or because he wanted an excuse to touch her?

He dropped his hand. 'Why are you afraid of him?'

'It doesn't matter.' Her mouth flattened.

'Did he visit you behind bars?' Had he threatened her?

'Him! Visit me? You've got to be kidding. In five years my only visitors were a couple of criminologists writing a book on female offenders and crimes of passion.' Sarcasm dripped from her voice. 'They found me such a *fascinating* study.'

She shouldered away from him, into the sun. Yet she rubbed her hands up her arms as if to warm herself.

Stunned, he let himself be distracted. In five years she'd had no personal visitors? What about her family and friends? Then he remembered the tawdry exposé interview with her stepmother. Lucy's family relationships were strained. But to be alone so long?

He felt no triumph, only regret as he read her grim tension, the way she battled not to show emotion.

'Tell me, Lucy.' His voice was gruff. 'Why are you afraid of Bruno Scarlatti?'

His gaze held hers and almost he thought he'd won. That she trusted him enough to tell him.

She shrugged but the movement was stiff as if her muscles had seized up. 'We agreed not to talk about the past. Let's abide by that. You wouldn't appreciate what I have to say.'

She turned towards the water.

There was no point trying to force her to talk. She'd proved time and again that she didn't bow to pressure.

But her terror couldn't be denied.

Something had happened. Something that frightened one of the most composed, self-sufficient women he knew.

He thought of her evidence at the trial. She'd claimed it was Bruno Scarlatti, not Sandro, who'd come to her room that night. He'd heard about the scene between Sandro and Lucy when earlier that day she'd pleaded for immediate leave to visit her sick father. Understandably, Sandro had refused, concerned that with Pia unwell and the nanny off work due to illness, they needed the au pair, Lucy.

The meeting had ended with Lucy shouting she'd find a way to leave despite her contract.

Her story was that Bruno had said he'd help her persuade the boss to give her leave and she'd innocently let him into her room. Once inside, he'd allegedly attacked her, tried to rape her. Sandro had heard the noise and come to her aid, but in the scuffle with Bruno he'd knocked his head against the antique fireplace and died.

Domenico rubbed a hand over his tense jaw, remembering all the holes in her story. The court had dismissed it. There was too much evidence of her guilt.

Pia had given evidence, backed by diary notes, that Sandro and Lucy had had a passionate affair. Bruno's evidence had been the same. He'd revealed her as a seductive tease who knew her power over men and bragged about twisting the boss around her little finger. He'd seen her and Sandro together, given dates and times.

Sandro had given her expensive treats, like the exquisite jewellery found in her room the night he died. The household had heard her threaten Sandro when he'd refused to let her go.

That night he'd been drinking, torn no doubt between concern for his wife and the fight with his mistress. He'd gone to Lucy's room with an expensive gift to salve her anger. But they'd fought again, she'd shoved him and, unsteady on his feet, he'd fallen and cracked his skull. As for Lucy blaming Bruno—he had an alibi.

Pia had found Sandro bleeding to death, cradled in Lucy's arms.

Domenico shivered, recalling the moment he'd discovered Lucy's identity—the image of her in a bloodstained nightdress with a blanket around her shoulders, being escorted to a police car outside the palazzo. Sandro was dead and she'd been arrested.

Domenico hadn't even been able to blame Sandro for his fatal attraction to the young Englishwoman. He knew how difficult Pia could be and guessed that in the months following childbirth she'd been particularly demanding.

More importantly, Domenico had first-hand experience of Lucy's power. He'd fallen under her spell in just a few hours. What must it have been like for Sandro, facing such temptation in his own home every day? That didn't excuse the affair. But Sandro was only human.

Who was Domenico to judge when he'd felt attraction sizzle the moment he'd looked into Lucy Knight's eyes? That knowledge had twisted guilt deep in his gut ever since.

He shifted his focus to the woman walking along

the beach. Her head was bowed and her arms were wrapped tight around her body.

Confusion filled him as he recalled the fear that had racked her as he'd held her.

Because she thought she'd seen Bruno Scarlatti. *Because he'd killed Sandro?*

The thought stopped the breath in Domenico's lungs. It wasn't possible. The court had been through all the evidence, right down to Lucy's fingerprints on the expensive necklace Sandro had given her that night. It had been a lovers' quarrel. And there was a witness who put Scarlatti elsewhere when Sandro died.

And yet… Again that frisson of unease stirred. That sense that something wasn't right.

Domenico forced himself to concentrate on proven facts. The evidence supported Lucy's guilt yet she was scared of Scarlatti. Had one part of her story been true? Had he tried to force himself on her?

There'd been an avid hunger in Scarlatti's eyes whenever he'd looked across the courtroom at Lucy. Domenico had noticed immediately, ashamed as he was of his own response to her.

Domenico's hands clenched so hard he found himself shaking. Could that be it? The idea hollowed his belly.

He wished Scarlatti was here now. Domenico needed an outlet for his churning fury.

'Scarlatti no longer works for the Volpe family.'

Lucy spun to find Domenico a few paces away, eyes shaded by wraparound sunglasses. She felt at a disadvantage, wondering what the lenses hid from view.

'Why not?'

'He was dismissed years ago. Rocco found evidence that he'd…bothered one of the maids.'

'Bothered?' Why wasn't she surprised? Bruno was a slime ball who wouldn't take no for an answer.

'She complained he was pestering her. A bit of digging revealed she wasn't the first.'

Lucy bit her lip. The temptation to spill her own story about Bruno was strong. But Domenico had heard it in court. He hadn't believed it then and wouldn't now. Defeat tasted sour on her tongue.

Why should it matter after all this time that he didn't believe her? Instead of getting easier to bear, it grew harder.

Nothing had changed. She'd let herself be lulled into believing it had.

Domenico was weakening her, subtly undermining her ability to keep the unsympathetic world at bay.

'Don't worry, he's long gone.'

She nodded. What was there to say?

'Now, let's get out on the water.'

'I've changed my mind. I'll stay ashore.'

'Why? So you can hide in your room and brood?'

Lucy's eyes widened. 'I *never* hide!'

'Isn't that what you're doing now?'

She knew Domenico's tactic. He deliberately baited her, yet she couldn't resist the challenge. The one thing, the only thing she'd had on her side all these years had been her resolute strength. An ability to tough out the worst the criminal justice system could throw at her and pretend it didn't matter.

She'd forced herself to morph from a scared, desperate teenager into a woman who could look after herself no matter what.

There was more than pride at stake. It was her faith in her one tangible asset—strength in the face of adversity.

Without that, how could she face the future that loomed like a black hole? She had no family now. No friends. No prospects, as each day's job-hunting proved. If she let herself weaken she'd never survive.

Lucy met Domenico's gaze, reading anticipation

in his stillness. He expected her to make a run for it, damn him.

'Where's your boat?'

Three hours later she was a different woman. The mutinous set of her mouth had eased into a smile that made Domenico's belly flip over. Her haunted expression had disappeared. Now her eyes shone pure forget-me-not blue, rivalling the sky for brightness.

He'd only once before seen a woman lit from within like this. It had been Lucy then too. Her enthusiasm was contagious.

He shook his head, unable to believe her avid enthusiasm was anything but real this time. There'd been no primping, not even a comb or mirror in the bag she'd brought. No coy looks or subtle feminine blandishments. Her focus had been on the boat and the sensation of speed as they circled the island. Her husky laughter still echoed in his ears. She'd been like a kid on a roller coaster for the first time—delighted and delightful in her glee.

'Did you *see* the size of that octopus?' She surfaced beside him, grinning as she removed the snorkel's mouthpiece. 'It's amazing, and the way it moves!'

'Do you like octopus? I could catch it for our dinner.' Like a smitten youth showing off for a pretty girl. Like the man he'd been that first day in Rome. He'd turned from a cabinet of ornate jewellery and fallen into the cerulean depths of her gaze.

Yet even that thought couldn't dim Domenico's good mood. He'd enjoyed the last couple of hours more than any he could remember in months.

She was a pleasure to be with. Her questions had stimulated rather than bored him. She'd made him see the place through fresh, appreciative eyes.

How long since he'd enjoyed such simple pleasures? Usually when he visited he was busy, finishing work or entertaining guests who were too sophisticated to get excited about snorkelling or a speedboat ride.

'No.' She reached out and put a restraining hand on his shoulder when he would have dived back under. 'Thank you, but I'd rather you let it be.'

'Squeamish about seeing your dinner before it appears on your plate?' He kept his eyes on her face though it was her slim hand on his shoulder that stole his attention.

'Maybe.' Her smile turned wistful. 'Can't we just leave him alone? Free?'

Something about the way she said that last word made him pause. Was that what she'd enjoyed so much? The freedom of their afternoon on the water?

It struck him that this was a massive change from the restrictions she'd known behind bars. He couldn't imagine such a life. How had she coped?

He wasn't in the business of feeling sorry for her. Yet seeing her so different from the touchy, self-protective woman he'd known, Domenico couldn't completely suppress a sense of connection between them.

His motive in being with her had been to soften her into accepting his deal—her silence for a big chunk of money. But somewhere in the past days he'd found himself *wanting* her company. He'd told himself he needed to understand the woman who threatened his family, but that wasn't all. Not any more.

He wanted to be with her. He wanted…

'In that case we'll leave it be.' He looked at the westering sun. 'It's time to stop. Come on.'

Lucy wrapped an oversized beach towel around herself, conscious of Domenico's gaze lingering as he'd helped her aboard. His eyes had shone silver as he took in the swimsuit moulding her body. It had only been for a second before he'd looked away, but that had ignited a slow, curling heat inside. His look had seared her to the core and shivers still rippled across her skin.

The trouble was, though they were on opposing sides, the old attraction was back, stronger than before.

Worse, she'd begun to *like* him.

He put her at ease and made her smile, and it wasn't just about him trying to persuade her to sign his contract. There was the way he was with little Chiara—like an honorary uncle instead of the man who employed half her family. The way he treated Lucy—always straight down the line. The way he'd held her this afternoon.

It scared her how much his concern had meant to her.

'Why did you never speak to me at the trial?'

Horrified, she heard the words slip out. Did she really want to break the afternoon's spell by dredging up the past? It seemed she did. 'I thought you'd talk to me at least. Acknowledge me.'

There. It was out in the open finally.

She turned her gaze on him. To her amazement, colour flushed his tanned face, rising high on those lean cheeks.

'Would it have changed anything?'

Lucy's lips firmed. It wouldn't have changed the trial's outcome but it would have meant everything to her.

'When I saw you there I thought you'd come to

support me.' Her mouth twisted. She'd felt utterly alone, her family so far away. 'Until I found out who you were.'

His eyes widened, something like shock tensing his face.

'Surely you knew that already.'

'How could I? I only knew your first name, remember?'

They'd had such a short time together, less than a day. Her chest tightened. It wasn't his fault she'd fallen under his spell so utterly. That she'd read too much into simple attraction. She'd been so inexperienced. Domenico was the first man to make her heart flutter.

She looked into his stunned eyes and realised what a little fool she'd been. What had her claim on him been? An afternoon's pleasant company compared with supporting his family in crisis.

All this time she'd blamed him for not hearing her out. How could he, with Pia clinging hysterically to him? With the weight of his brother's death weighing him down?

How could she have expected him to leave those responsibilities for her, a woman he barely knew? Simply because she'd woven juvenile fantasies about him! Suddenly she felt a million years older than the immature girl who'd stood in the dock.

She raised her hand when he went to speak.

'Forget it, Domenico. It doesn't matter now.' To her surprise, it was true. Clinging to pain only held her back.

If this afternoon had shown her one thing it was that life was worth living—here, now. She intended to grab it by the throat and make the most of it. No point repining over what couldn't be changed.

'I'm thirsty. Do you have anything?'

Still Domenico stared, a strange arrested look in his eyes. 'There's beer or soft drink.' He stepped closer and now it wasn't his expression that held her.

He'd wiped the excess water away but hadn't wrapped a towel around himself. She drank in the sight of his gold-toned body, powerfully muscled and mouth-wateringly tempting. His low-slung board shorts emphasised his virile masculinity.

'Juice?' she croaked.

He poured her a glass then collected a beer and sat down.

'We're not going ashore?'

He shrugged and Lucy couldn't help but watch the way muscle and sinew moved across his shoulders and chest. In Rome he wore a suit like a man bred for formal dress. But his tailored clothes hid a body that spoke to her on the deepest, most elemental level. A level that made her forget herself.

'Not unless you're in a rush. Sunset over the island looks terrific from here. I thought you'd enjoy it.'

Lucy had no doubt she would, if she could tear her eyes from him.

'Thank you for this afternoon,' she said brightly. 'I've never done anything like this before.' Better to babble, she decided, than to gawk silently. Why didn't he cover himself?

'You've never been snorkelling?'

'Or for a ride in a speedboat. I've never been in a boat.'

His eyebrows rose. 'Never?'

Lucy smiled. She couldn't help it. His look of amazement was priceless. 'I'm a landlubber. I've never even been in a canoe.'

'But you can swim.'

'Even in England we've got public indoor pools, you know.' She paused. 'That's why I jumped at the chance to work in Italy, to see the Mediterranean.' Pleasure rose at the sight of the azure sea, the sky turning blush pink over Domenico's island and, when she turned, the dazzling view of villages clinging to the mainland.

It was the embodiment of those fantasies she'd had as a girl: sun, sand and an exotic foreign location. Even a sun-bronzed hunk with mesmerising good looks.

How naïve she'd been, yearning for adventure.

'You lived far from the sea?'

She sipped her juice. 'Not far. But our interests were all on dry land.'

'Our?'

'My dad and me.' She paused, registering the familiar pang of loss, but with her attention on the breathtaking view, the pain wasn't as sharp as usual. 'He was a bus driver and mad about vintage cars. I spent my childhood visiting displays of old automobiles or helping him fix ours.' She smiled. 'He'd have loved that one you have at the palazzo.'

Her smile faded and her throat tightened as it often did when she thought of her dad and the precious time they'd lost. 'He died just after the trial.'

She turned to find Domenico looking as grim as she'd ever seen him. This time the shiver that ran through her wasn't one of pleasure but chill foreboding.

'I'm sorry for your loss, Lucy.' He stood and moved towards her, then shifted abruptly away.

'It's no one's fault,' she murmured, refusing to listen to the little voice that said she should have found some way to see her beloved dad before he passed on. The voice of guilt, reminding her of all she'd put him through when he was so ill.

'But you wanted to be with him.'

Surprised, she looked up and saw understanding in his eyes. Of course. He'd been overseas when his brother had died. He knew how it felt to be far away at such a time.

'Yes.' Her voice was hoarse.

'He would have known. He would have understood.'

'I know, but it doesn't make it easier, does it?'

He was silent so long she thought she'd overstepped the mark, referring however obliquely to his own loss.

'No, it doesn't.' His mouth twisted. 'I was in New York when Sandro died. I kept telling myself it would never have happened if I'd been in Rome.'

Lucy bit her lip but finally let the words escape. 'It wouldn't have made any difference.' Did he want to hear that from the woman he thought responsible?

His eyes darkened, then he nodded. 'You're right. It's just that Sandro was—' he frowned '—special. Our parents died when I was young and Sandro was more than a big brother.'

'He was a good man,' she said. He hadn't been perfect. She'd wished he'd got specialist help for his wife's depression. Yet though she didn't agree, she understood his reluctance not to upset her when she saw outside help as proof she was a bad mother.

As an employer he'd been decent. Looking back, she realised what a quandary she'd put him in with her hysterical demand to leave immediately for England. Of course he'd put his family's needs first. She'd been young and overwrought, convinced a delay of a few days would make a difference to her father.

'Sandro was the one who taught me to swim, and to snorkel.' Domenico smiled wistfully. 'And, come to that, how to drive a speedboat.'

'My dad taught me how to strip down an engine.' Her mouth curved reminiscently. 'And how to make a kite and fly it. He even came to ballet classes when I was little and too shy to go alone.'

'He sounds like a perfect father.'

'He was.'

'You never wanted to be a mechanic or a driver like him?'

'No. I wanted to be a teacher. Working with children was always my dream. But that's not possible now.' She kept her voice brisk, refusing to wallow in self-pity.

'What will you do?' He sounded grave, as if her answer mattered.

Lucy looked at the sunset glowing amber and peach, rimmed with gold, then across to the mainland, where the dying sun gilded the coastline into something fantastic. It was the most exquisite view. She stored the memory against the empty days ahead, when life would be all struggle.

'I took a bookkeeping course. I thought there'd be more chance of getting a job working with figures than with people, given my record.' Except she doubted she'd be left alone long enough to find a job. This was a temporary respite. Once she left, the press would hound her. Who would employ her?

Abruptly she put her glass down and stood. 'Isn't it time we headed back?' She needed to be alone, to sort out the problems she'd avoided while she was here. She'd been living in a fantasy world. Soon she'd face reality.

Lucy spun away. But the deck was slick where she'd dripped seawater. Her foot shot out beneath her. She flailed but was falling when Domenico grabbed her and hauled her to him.

She told herself it was the shock of almost falling that made adrenalin surge and her heart thump. It had nothing to do with the look in Domenico's stormy eyes or the feel of his hot, damp body against hers.

'You can let me go.' Her breasts rose and fell with her choppy breathing.

Lucy put her hands on his arms to push herself away. Instead her fingers curled around the tensile strength of his biceps as if protesting the need to move.

'What if I don't want to let you go?' His voice was so deep its vibration rumbled through her.

Bent back over his arm, she watched his face come closer. His gaze moved to her mouth and her heart gave a mighty leap as she read his intent.

'No!' Her voice was breathless. 'I don't want this!'

He shook his head. 'I thought we'd agreed, Lucy. No more lies.' For a moment longer he watched her, waiting for the protest they both knew she wouldn't make.

Then slowly, deliberately, he lowered his head.

CHAPTER EIGHT

DOMENICO'S LIPS BRUSHED hers in a light, barely there caress that made her mouth tingle and her blood surge. Twice, three times, he rubbed his mouth across hers, sending every sense into overdrive, till finally impatience overwhelmed caution and she clamped her hands to his wet hair and kissed him back.

There! No more teasing, just the heat of his mouth on hers. Her fingers slid around his skull, cradling him. The reality of him, the unyielding strength of bone and bunched muscle, of surprisingly soft lips making her blood sing, was everything she'd imagined and more.

His tongue slipped along the seam of her lips and it was the most natural thing in the world to open for him. For him to delve into her mouth and swirl delight through her veins. For her to respond with an honesty that eclipsed any vague thought of restraint.

She felt as if she'd waited a lifetime for this.

It didn't matter that she was a novice and he a master at this art. Eagerness made up for inexperience as she met his need with her own. Their tongues tangled, slid, stroked and goose bumps broke out across her flesh.

Domenico sucked her tongue into his mouth and her pulse catapulted. He nipped her bottom lip and Lucy sighed as pleasure engulfed her.

She leaned back, supported only by his embrace but she had no fear of falling. His arms were like steel ropes, lashing her close. His chest slid against hers and she gasped as electricity sparked and fired through her body, to her nipples, her stomach, the apex of her thighs. Behind the shocking heat came a melting languor that liquefied her bones and stole her will.

She tilted her head, accommodating him as desire escalated and their kisses grew urgent, hungry. She was burning up and so was he, his flesh on fire beneath her hands.

Yes! This was what she wanted from him, had always wanted. Even when she'd spat and snarled, she'd fought this chemistry between them.

Why had she tried to fight it? It was delicious, addictive.

Domenico tasted of the sea and dark, wickedly rich chocolate—a seductive mix. She shivered in sensual overload as he devoured her with a thoroughness that matched every long-suppressed need.

Had he yearned for this too? Had he lain awake, imagining this moment?

The slide of their bodies was pure magic. The thin fabric of her swimsuit was negligible against the heated promise of his body. Lucy pressed closer, revelling in his powerful musculature, the heady scent of his skin and a deeper, musky note of arousal.

He kissed her throat and she arched back, feeling her feminine power even as she knew herself caught in a web of desire. She was utterly open to his caresses, unprotected against his strength. Yet Lucy felt no doubt or fear. Each kiss he pressed to her skin was homage to the spell woven between them.

Rousing herself from drugged delight, Lucy pulled herself higher, rubbing her cheek against his. The friction of his sandpapery jaw sent another shaft of lightning straight to her groin and she shivered in delicious arousal.

She nipped his ear lobe and heard him growl, low in his throat. It was the sexiest thing she'd ever heard. She smiled and did it again, eager at the thought of Domenico reacting to her at the most primal level.

Large hands wrapped around her waist and he lifted her high to sit on something. Domenico pushed her thighs apart and stepped between them, lodging himself at her core.

'Domenico.' Her voice was a rasp of pleasure as the fire spread, overriding a belated voice of warning.

She wanted him. Had done for so long. Even in the days when she'd hated him, she'd secretly yearned for this delight. This affirmation. She'd given up trying to puzzle the attraction that smouldered between them. It was enough to let glorious pleasure sweep her away.

Lucy felt the power of his erection between her legs and against her belly and her breath faltered. They felt so *right* together. It was all she could do not to rock against him, lost in the need for sensual satisfaction.

With an effort of willpower that almost undid her, she opened her eyes and met the mercurial glitter of his. Heat and shimmering silver fire engulfed her.

His hand palmed her breast and she gasped, overloaded with exquisite sensation. It was too much to bear.

She grabbed his neck and pulled him to her, wanting his lips on hers. Needing the dark mystery of their kisses. Needing *him*.

Long fingers thrust through her hair, tipping her head back as he tasted her in a long, luxurious kiss that curled her toes. His other hand teased her nipple. Darts of heat arced from the spot, making her move restlessly.

Immediately Domenico slid his hand from her scalp, down her spine, to splay over her bottom and drag her up tight against him. He kissed her hard, his tongue delving as his blatantly aroused body surged against hers.

The world tumbled and re-formed. Her blood sizzled like molten metal swirling in a crucible of pure need. Her lips moved against his and her dazed brain almost stopped functioning.

Domenico eased away a fraction as he slipped his hand over her bare thigh to brush the Lycra at the juncture of her thighs. A bolt of lightning slashed through her, jolting every nerve end, concentrating every sense on that point of contact. She grabbed his shoulders.

Wide-eyed she looked up. His face was pared to austere lines that spoke of raw hunger. Gone was his sophistication, stripped to something more elemental.

More dangerous. The words surfaced in her foggy brain as long fingers teased the band of fab-

ric at her inner thighs, sending whorls of fiery pleasure through her.

Desire warred with shock as she realised how
far their kisses had taken her. To the brink of ful-
filment. To the brink of giving herself to the man
she'd called enemy. To the point of baring herself
emotionally as well as physically. *That* was what
scared her.

Her hand clamped his as he moved to insinu-
ate his fingers under the fabric. He froze, his eyes
turning blindly to hers. His other hand still cupped
her breast.

Lucy watched realisation dawn. His eyes lost that
unfocused glitter and widened a fraction.

'I think it's time to stop.'

It was a wonder he heard. Her voice was hoarse,
a frayed thread of sound. Yet he understood. An
instant later he'd backed away, his hands furrowing
through his thick hair as if he didn't trust himself
not to touch her again.

Lucy swayed, perched on the edge of the boat.
Without his support she felt bereft. She bit her
tongue to stop herself calling him back. Her eyes
ate him up, from the hard jut of his jaw to the dusting of hair across his broad pectoral muscles and
the swell of his biceps as he lifted his arms. From

the heavy arousal to the storm-dark glint of his hooded eyes.

She wanted him still. Wanted him to step back and obliterate her doubts with the caress of that clever mouth, seduce her into delight with that big, hard body. Every nerve ending danced in anticipation, undermining her resolve.

Fear surfaced. She'd never known how compelling the need for sexual gratification could be. Domenico tempted her to forget everything. She'd thought herself strong and self-sufficient. Yet all it had taken was one kiss to undo every barrier she'd spent years erecting.

What did it mean?

'You're right. It's late.' He turned away and, to her consternation, Lucy felt disappointment swell.

After an evening apart breakfast the next morning was full of silences and stilted conversation.

What had got into him?

Oh, he knew what had got into him. He'd desired Lucy from the moment he'd set eyes on her all those years ago.

How could he have come so close to sex, raw and unvarnished, with the woman convicted of killing Sandro? Guilt churned in his belly. Where was his family loyalty?

Gone the moment he held her. Evicted by sexual desire and the conviction Lucy Knight was a mystery he'd just begun to unravel. An enigma who'd haunted him for years. He desperately needed to understand her for his peace of mind.

It wasn't only desire she triggered. He'd been beside himself with thwarted fury when he realised she'd been attacked by a family employee. His need to protect had been as strong as if she was his responsibility. *His woman.*

A frisson of warning crept down his spine.

Yesterday's revelations had rocked him to the core.

For years he'd believed Lucy had engineered their initial meeting. How unlikely a coincidence that she'd literally bump into him, on his fleeting visit to Rome, when she already worked for his brother?

When the revelations had come thick and fast about Sandro's uncharacteristic weakness for his au pair, the way she'd twisted him round her little finger and milked him for expensive gifts, it hadn't taken a genius to work out she'd tried out the same wiles on Domenico.

He'd picked up the tension in his brother's household that very morning on his visit, only later realising it was due to a love triangle.

Or was it?

She'd said yesterday she hadn't known his identity before the trial. It was tempting to think Lucy lied but there was no reason now. Besides, he'd seen real hurt in her face when she'd asked why he'd avoided her. Hell! He no longer knew what to believe.

Could she be innocent?

His blood froze. The idea that he'd misjudged her so badly, letting her suffer for a crime she didn't commit, didn't bear thinking about.

He looked across to where she sat, eyes riveted on her breakfast as if it fascinated her.

Never before had she refused to meet his eyes.

He wanted to demand she look at him. He wanted to kiss that sultry down-turned mouth and unleash the passion that had blasted the back off his skull yesterday. Behind that reserve lurked a woman unlike any he'd known. More alive, more vital, more dangerous.

Was he out of control, ignoring what he owed his dead brother? Or were his doubts valid?

'Mail, sir.' The maid entered with a bundle of letters. To his surprise she placed an envelope beside Lucy's plate.

'For me?' Lucy frowned. 'Thank you.'

Who knew she was here? Someone she'd corresponded with via email? He forced himself to take another sip of fresh juice rather than demand to know who'd sent it.

She slipped a finger under the seal and withdrew a sheet of paper, discarding the envelope. That was when he saw a bold, too-familiar logo. It belonged to the magazine that had run her stepmother's interview.

He clenched his jaw, forcing down bile. Obviously Lucy was making the most of her opportunities, accepting his hospitality while negotiating with the gutter press for a better financial deal.

It shouldn't surprise him.

So why did he feel betrayed?

So much for the wronged innocent. How often would he let her dupe him?

'Is it a better offer?'

'Sorry?' Lucy looked up into eyes of gun-metal grey, piercing in their intensity.

She blinked, stunned by the change in Domenico. His eyebrows slashed in a V of disapproval and he looked as if he'd bitten something sour.

True, she'd shied away from contact this morning, still shocked by her response yesterday. But there'd been no venom in his voice, no ice in his stare when she'd entered the breakfast room.

'I assume from your absorption they're offering better terms than I did.'

Belatedly understanding dawned as he stared at the paper in her hand.

Pain sliced down, sharp as a blade of ice. It tore through her heart, shredding the bud of hope she'd nursed since yesterday. Making a mockery of that warm, sunshine glow Domenico had put there with his protectiveness, his acceptance and his desire.

What an idiot she'd been! How pathetically gullible.

Hadn't life taught her not to believe in miracles?

Domenico Volpe caring for her, trusting her even a little, would be a miracle. Yet against the odds she'd hoped some of the emotions she'd read in him yesterday had been real.

She'd almost given herself to him!

Lucy cringed at how far she'd let herself be conned.

Crazy, but even more than his sexual hunger or his protectiveness, Lucy missed their camaraderie as they'd snorkelled and watched the sunset. The sense of acceptance and liking. That had been precious. They'd shared things that were important to them both. Memories of their loved ones.

For those few hours Lucy had felt genuine warmth, a spark of liking. Of trust.

Fool, fool, fool. He'd buttered her up to get what he wanted.

'I said—'

'I heard.' She looked from him to the letter in her clenched fingers. There was nothing to choose between them. At least the press was upfront about what they wanted. Domenico had tried to distract her with a show of friendliness.

And she'd fallen for it.

What was one more deceit in a world of disappointment? Yet this one gouged pain in a heart she'd told herself was too well protected to hurt again.

'It's an attractive offer,' she said at last. As if the idea of selling her story to those hyenas didn't make her flesh crawl. They'd done more than destroy her reputation. They'd harried her poor dad in his last weeks. 'I'll have to consider it carefully.'

Distaste burned but maybe she didn't have the luxury of saying no any more. If she sold her story she'd get enough to start fresh. Hadn't she earned the right to profit after the terrible price she'd paid?

Maybe if she co-operated they'd leave her alone and she could pretend to be the woman she'd been before.

And pigs might fly. The press would never let her go whilst there was a story to be sold. Lucy squeezed her eyes shut, imagining lurid revelations about her attempts to live a normal life. Shocked reactions from neighbours when they discovered a killer living in their midst.

It would never end. Not for years.

She snapped open her eyes and glared as Domenico looked down his aristocratic nose at her.

A silent howl of despair rose. She'd wanted to trust him. She'd begun to open up, to believe he cared.

'Perhaps I could canvass the other media outlets and see what they're offering.'

His scowl was a balm to her lacerated feelings. Let him stew!

'You haven't already done that? Isn't that why you spend so long on the computer? Negotiating the best deal?'

'Actually, no. But of course you won't believe me.'

He leaned across the table, his eyes flashing daggers. 'If you haven't contacted the press, how do they know where you are?'

Lucy shoved her chair back and stood.

'Perhaps they took an educated guess,' she purred. 'Since they knew I was at your palazzo it wouldn't take much to suppose I'd be at one of your properties. Maybe they've written to me at each one. Who knows? Maybe this is the first of a flurry of offers.' She smiled, injecting saccharine sweetness into her tone. 'A bidding war. Wouldn't that be fun?'

He looked as if he wanted to strangle her with his bare hands. They clenched into massive fists before him.

Lucy's bravado ended as she recalled the stroke of those hands across her body. He'd touched her as if she were the most precious thing on earth.

She'd *felt* precious, desirable, special.

She forced down welling pain.

'Here.' She slowed as she walked past, letting the letter flutter to his lap. 'See what the opposition is offering. Maybe you'll increase your bid.'

Lucy strode out of the door before nausea engulfed her.

'Excuse me, boss. Have you seen Chiara?'

Domenico looked up from his email to find Rocco at the door, concern etched on his face.

'Isn't she with Lucy? They spend half the day together.'

'Chiara said Miss Lucy couldn't play today. She said she looked upset.' He paused and Domenico's stomach dipped. A finger of guilt slid across his neck as he remembered the pain he'd seen on Lucy's face when he'd confronted her.

After what they'd shared yesterday, and in light of what they'd *almost* shared, her anguish had been a knife to his gut. It made him feel like a jerk. Even though he was trying to protect his family, he'd been in the wrong.

Maybe because his anger wasn't about protecting his nephew but himself? Because he'd overreacted when he'd seen her correspondence as he'd felt his illusions shatter?

Lucy Knight got under his skin as no other woman. He'd lashed out because emotion had overridden his brain.

Certainty had become doubt. But was it because he wanted her for himself or because she was innocent? He circled again and again round the puzzling truths he'd discovered about her.

She had him so confounded he didn't know what to believe. He'd felt so betrayed this morning, discovering he couldn't rely on his instincts where she was concerned.

Then he'd read the letter and realised she'd told the truth. The magazine had taken a chance on finding her here.

He'd been boorish and in the wrong. The knowledge didn't sit well.

'Chiara didn't come in for lunch.' Rocco interrupted his troubled musings.

'That's not like her.' Domenico frowned, anxiety stirring.

'No. She hasn't been seen in any of her usual haunts for hours. I'm just about to search for her.'

'Where's Lucy?' Domenico shoved his chair back.

'She's already searching.'

Most of the staff was scouring the shoreline, though no one had voiced their deepest fears, that Chiara had got out of her depth in the water. Domenico strode along the path at the wilderness end of the island, knowing someone had to check the less obvious places. That was how he ran into Lucy. Literally. She catapulted around a curve in the track and into his arms.

Domenico grasped her close. The summer sun lit her hair to gold and he inhaled her sweet fragrance. Yesterday he'd imprinted her body on his memory and now he didn't want to let her go. Crazy at it seemed, it felt as if she belonged there against him.

'Please,' she gasped, her hand splaying against his chest. It trembled. 'Please, help me.'

'Lucy?' He tilted her head up. 'What is it?'

She was breathless, barely able to talk. Her cheeks were flushed and there was dirt smeared across her cheek as if she'd fallen. Domenico tensed.

'Is it Chiara?'

She nodded. 'Up ahead.' She grabbed his shirt as

he made to go. 'No! Wait.' She gulped in air and he forced himself to wait till she could speak.

'You'll be faster than me. We need rope and a torch. A medical kit too.'

'The well?' His heart plunged into a pool of icy fear.

'No. A sinkhole. I found her hair ribbon on the edge of it and some marbles.'

Domenico's breath stopped. If she'd been playing too close to the edge and then leaned in…

'I'll go and check it out.'

Lucy shook her head, her hands clutching like talons. 'No! I've done that. There's no sound from below. We need a rope to reach her. Every minute counts. Please, trust me on this.' He read her desperation.

He thought of the way she'd cared for Chiara as they played together, and her careful nurturing of Taddeo all those years ago.

He couldn't waste precious time. He had to trust her judgement. A second later he was gone, pounding down the dusty path to the villa.

When he returned, laden with supplies, Lucy had disappeared. He found her half a kilometre on, at the edge of the narrow hole. She was leaning down, talking. As he sprinted to her he realised she was telling a story about a brave princess called Chiara who was rescued in her hour of need.

'She's spoken to you?' He shrugged off the rope looped across his shoulder and put down the medical kit.

Lucy's face was solemn. 'No. But I thought if she comes to and hears a familiar voice she won't be so scared.' Her mouth was white-rimmed and she blinked hard. Domenico squeezed her shoulder.

'Thank you, Lucy. That's a great idea.' He wasn't sure he'd have thought of it.

'Where are the others?' She looked beyond him.

'Still at the shore. They'll be here soon. Chiara's grandmother will have got the message to them by now.' He looked around. 'I'll have to tie this to that old olive tree. You keep a look out while I'm down there.'

'No. I'll go.'

Domenico dropped to his knees and shone the torch down the hole but he couldn't see anything. His heart sank but he quickly uncoiled the rope.

'I said I'll go down.' As if he'd let her risk her neck down there. 'My property. My risk.'

'Have you seen the size of that hole? Your shoulders are too wide. You'll never fit.'

Domenico turned to scrutinise the sinkhole.

Damn! She was right. In his youth he'd done some

caving but the squeezes had become difficult as he'd grown. This hole was so narrow he wasn't sure a grown woman could get down.

Nevertheless he opened his mouth to protest.

Lucy's fingers pressed his lips. He tasted dust and salt and the familiar sweet flavour of her skin. His nostrils filled with her scent. Despite the crisis his body tightened.

'Don't argue, Domenico. If I'd come out to play with her this morning this wouldn't have happened.'

'It's not your fault.' Already he was looping the rope around her, securing it firmly. 'You didn't do anything wrong.'

Deep blue eyes met his and a flash of something passed between them. Something that pounded through his chest and into his soul.

'Thank you, Domenico. But that's how it feels. Now, how do I lower myself?'

'Don't worry. I'll take care of it all.'

The next hour was pure nightmare for Lucy. She'd never been fond of small, dark places and being confined in a claustrophobically narrow hole evoked panicked memories of her first nights behind bars, when life had been an unreal horror.

She scraped off skin getting through the entrance but to her relief, the hole widened as she progressed.

Even better, she found Chiara conscious, though barely. Lucy's heart sped as she heard her whimper.

'It's all right, sweetie. You're safe.'

Nevertheless it took an age. First to undo the rope so Domenico could send down the medical kit. Then to assess Chiara's injuries—grazes, a nasty bump and a broken wrist. Then to bind her wrist and reassure her while she secured the thick rope around her.

Lucy wished she could go up and hold her close but there wasn't room for two. Finally, an age later, she tugged the rope so Domenico could lift Chiara free. Lucy bit her lip, hoping her assessment of minor injuries was right. They couldn't leave her here much longer; already she was shivering from shock and cold. Goodness knew how long it would take to get a medic from the mainland.

The shadows had lengthened and the sky clouded over by the time Lucy entrusted herself again to Domenico's strong arms. She was breathless with relief as he hauled her up to sit on the ground. A crowd of people was there, huddled around Chiara.

Lucy gulped lungfuls of sweet air, hardly daring believe she was on the surface again.

'How is she?' Her voice sounded rusty.

'She'll be fine, but she's going to the mainland for a check up.' The deep voice came from close by. Powerful arms pulled her higher then wrapped her close. A sense of belonging filled her, and sheer relief as she sank into Domenico's hold.

Weakness invaded her bones and Lucy let her head drop against his chest. Just while she collected herself. Her heart pounded out of sync as she breathed deep, absorbing the peace she found in his embrace.

How could it be? He'd berated and duped her. He'd raised her up till she felt like a goddess in his arms, then reduced her almost to tears with cruel taunts.

Her body betrayed her. It never wanted to move again.

Dimly she became aware of noise and lifted her head to applause and cheers. They were all looking at her, smiling and clapping.

'Thank you, Lucy.' Rocco came forward and, turning her in Domenico's arms, kissed her on both cheeks. 'You saved our special girl.'

His mother came next, the friendly woman who'd been so kind to her, then a string of others, some she knew and some she didn't. One by one they embraced her and kissed her cheeks. And all the while Domenico supported her as if he knew her shaky legs couldn't keep her upright unaided.

Warmth stirred. A warmth Lucy hadn't known

in what seemed a lifetime of cold, miserable isolation. It radiated out till her whole body tingled with
it. Something deep inside splintered and fell away,
like ice from a glacier. Its loss made her feel raw
and vulnerable and yet closer to these welcoming
people than she'd felt to anyone in years.

Finally they moved away, bustling around Chiara.

Lucy stayed in Domenico's arms, too exhausted,
too stunned to move. A smile stretched her muscles yet she felt the hot track of tears down her
cheeks. She didn't understand why she cried, but
she couldn't seem to stop. A sob filled her chest
then broke out, shocking her.

Domenico's arms tightened.

'It's all right, Lucy. We'll have you home soon.'

Home? Bitterness drenched her. She was the eter-
nal outsider. She had no home, nowhere to belong.
Then she stiffened. She had to get a grip.

Lucy blinked and saw Domenico looking down
at her, no arrogance, no hauteur, no accusation on
his face. There was an expression in his gleaming
eyes that made another splinter of ice crack away.
She shivered, realising how defenceless she was
against him now.

'Thank you, Lucy, for saving Chiara.' He lifted
his hand and wiped her cheek. She'd never seen him
look more serious. 'You risked your life for her.'

Lucy shook her head. 'Anyone would have—'

'No! Not anyone. Lots wouldn't have dared. If it hadn't been for you I dread to think how long it would have been before we found her and got her out.'

His thumb swiped her cheek again, then rubbed across her lip. She tasted the subtle spice of Domenico's skin through the salt tang of tears.

'I was wrong about you.' His voice had lost its mellow richness. Instead she heard strain. 'You're not the woman I thought. What I said this morning... I apologise.' He drew a deep breath. 'Can you forgive me?'

Numb with shock, Lucy nodded.

Then sweet wonder filled her as he dipped his head. Their gazes meshed, their breaths mingled and something like joy swelled in her breast.

Domenico leaned in and kissed her gently, tenderly, with a reverence that filled her heart with delight and eased her wounded soul.

CHAPTER NINE

'OF COURSE TADDEO is welcome here as usual. Nothing will ever change that. He's my nephew and as precious to me as a son.'

Domenico thrust his hand through his hair in frustration as his sister-in-law squawked her outrage down the phone line. She was family and, for his nephew's sake especially, Domenico put up with her.

'Yes, Lucy's here. Far better she stays here away from the press than selling her story. Isn't that what you wanted?'

He eased the phone from his ear as Pia unleashed a torrent of objections. Mouth flattening, he strode to the wide terrace and inhaled deep of the fresh sea air. Pia had read about Domenico rescuing Lucy from the press and demanded to know why she was still with him.

As if he had to clear his actions with Pia!

He'd only got involved in this situation because Pia had pleaded for him to intervene.

Though this had passed well beyond a simple business negotiation. He was…personally involved.

He thought of his overwhelming relief when Lucy had emerged from that dark hole. For heart-stopping minutes panic had filled him as it seemed to take a lifetime to haul her up. Domenico tasted rusty fear, remembering.

He'd gathered her close and hadn't been able to release her even when her well-wishers crowded around. He'd needed her with him.

Domenico scrubbed a hand over his jaw. He and Lucy had unfinished business. Business he'd delayed. It had nothing to do with Sandro or Pia or the press.

'Calm down, Pia, and hear me out.'

Lucy heard Domenico as she entered the house. She stopped, not to eavesdrop but because he had that effect on her. She'd given up pretending. She might be weak where he was concerned but she refused to lie to herself.

The sound of that rich macchiato voice pooled heat deep in her body. The memory of his tender kiss, as if he treasured her, made forbidden hope unfurl.

'I understand your concerns, Pia, but she's not the woman the press have painted.'

Lucy started, realising Domenico was talking to his sister-in-law about *her*. She went rigid, torn between curiosity and protecting herself. Since the rescue it had been hard to keep him at arm's length. Yet she needed to because he could hurt her badly.

She was moving away when he spoke again.

'That was years ago, Pia. People change. *She's* changed. Did you get her letter?'

Lucy's steps faltered.

'You shouldn't have destroyed it. She wrote to say how much she regretted Sandro's death. She was genuine, Pia. I'm sure of that.'

Lucy's heart hammered against her ribs, her hand clenching on the door handle.

Domenico was standing up for her against his sister-in-law! She could scarcely believe it.

'I understand, Pia. But it's time we moved on. For Taddeo's sake.' He paused as if listening. 'We can't change the past, much as we wish it. I know Lucy wishes she could. She's genuinely sorry for what happened to Sandro.'

Lucy clung to the door handle as her knees wobbled.

'That's your choice, Pia. But think about what I've said. Living in the present is the best thing for your son. He's a fine boy, one Sandro would have been proud of. You don't want him growing up bitter and fearful, do you?'

Domenico's voice dipped on his brother's name, reminding Lucy this was a private conversation.

She released the door and crossed the foyer. Confusion filled her but it didn't dim her smile and her step was light.

Domenico had stood up for her!

Sunlight filtered through spreading branches and Lucy leaned against her cushion with a sigh of contentment.

'More?' Domenico lifted a bunch of dark grapes with the bloom of the vineyard still on them.

'I couldn't.' She patted her stomach. 'I've eaten like a horse.'

His eyes followed the movement and fire licked her. She stiffened then forced herself to relax as his gaze grew intent. Domenico saw too much, especially now when her skill at hiding her feelings had disintegrated.

'I'll have some.' Chiara skipped across the clearing. The plaster on her wrist was the only reminder of last week's ordeal.

Lucy met Domenico's rueful gaze and realised they shared the same thought. She smiled, sharing the moment of relief, and he smiled back. It was like watching the sunrise after endless night, warming her with an inner glow.

Her breathing snagged then resumed, quicker and shorter as she watched his eyes darken. Her skin shivered as if responding to the phantom brush of his hand.

'Domi? Can't I have some?'

Domenico dragged his attention to Chiara. 'Of course, *bella*.' He handed over the bunch then leaned back on his arms. Lucy's heart pattered faster. If he shifted again they'd be touching.

Domenico hadn't touched her since Chiara's accident. That made her wonder if she'd imagined the strength of his embrace that day, or the way his hands had trembled as he held her. Her breath eased out in a sigh.

She'd never forget the magic of his kiss. Her fingers drifted to her mouth as she relived the brush of his lips.

It worried her how much she longed for him. How readily she responded now he treated her as a welcome guest. After hearing him defend her to Pia she hadn't been able to quell effervescent excitement, or the conviction that things had changed irrevocably between them.

She looked up to find his hooded eyes gleaming with heat. It arced between them, pulsing darts of sizzling awareness to her breasts, her belly and beyond.

Lucy shivered and his mouth curled in a lop-sided smile that carved a long dimple down his lean cheek. She curled her fingers into the grass, fighting the impulse to reach out and touch.

'So, Lucy.' He paused, glancing across to where Chiara sat with the flowers she'd gathered. 'You approve of Italian picnics?'

'I *adore* Italian picnics.'

'You've only been on one.'

She shrugged and felt the soft breeze waft over her bare arms, the melting laxness in her bones. 'What's not to like? Sunshine and food fresh from the farm.' She gestured to the remains of home baked bread, bowls of ricotta and local honey, pro-sciutto, olives and a cornucopia of summer fruits. 'It's heaven. Almost as good as our picnics back home.'

His eyebrows slanted high. 'Almost?'

'Well, there's nothing like a sudden English rain-storm to liven up outdoor eating.'

He laughed, the deep rich sound curling round her. An answering smile hovered on Lucy's mouth.

Smiling had become second nature lately. Be-cause she'd been made to feel she belonged. By Chi-ara's warm-hearted family and by Domenico. Gone was his judgemental frown, replaced by easy-going acceptance that banished so many shadows. He'd taken her snorkelling again, taught her to waterski and whiled away more hours than he needed to in her company, never once mentioning his brother or the story she might sell to the press. *As if he trusted her.*

Lucy could relax with him now.

No, that wasn't right. This tingling awareness wasn't relaxation. It was confidence and excitement and pleasure all rolled together.

Risky pleasure, when it lulled her into fantasy. When she found herself hoping the horrors of the past would vanish and leave them untroubled in this paradise.

A chill frisson snaked up her backbone.

It can't last.

One day soon the real world would intrude.

Lucy marvelled that Domenico had taken so much time out from what must be a heavy work schedule. He'd have business elsewhere. And she… she'd have to go too.

Regret lanced her and she twisted towards Chiara rather than let Domenico glimpse her pain.

Its intensity shocked her. It ripped through her, stealing the breath in her lungs.

Lucy pressed a hand to her chest.

'Are you okay?' Domenico moved abruptly as if sensing her discomfort.

'I'm fine.' This time her smile was a desperate lie. 'Just a little too much indulgence after all.'

Panic stirred. This wasn't just regret that the vacation was almost over. She'd known it would be tough trying to create a new life. She'd spent the last weeks facing the unpalatable facts of a future without family, friends, a job or anywhere to call home.

But the dread that made her skin break into a cold sweat owed nothing to that. It had everything to do with Domenico Volpe and what she'd begun to feel for him.

She felt…too much.

On a surge of frantic energy Lucy shot to her feet. Domenico was just as quick, his expression concerned as he broke his own unspoken rule and encircled her wrist with long fingers.

Instantly Lucy stilled, willing her pulse to slow.

'What is it, Lucy?'

'Nothing. I just wanted to move.'

Grey eyes searched her face and she held her breath, praying he couldn't read her thoughts. She could barely understand them herself. Amazing as it seemed, she *cared* for Domenico in a way that made the idea of leaving him send panic spurting through her.

'Liar.' To her addled brain the whisper sounded like a caress.

The stroke of his thumb against her wrist *was* a caress. She clamped her hand on his to stop it, looking down to see his dark golden fingers cradle her paler ones.

They held each other, fingers meshing. Strength throbbed through her. How could she give this up?

Because she must.

'You promised—'

'I promised not to revisit the past.' His breath was warm on her cheek. 'But this isn't about the past, is it, Lucy? This is about the present. Here. Now.'

Unable to stop herself, she turned her head and met his eyes. Molten heat poured through her as their gazes locked. The world receded, blocked out by the knowledge she read there, the awareness.

'I can't—' Words clogged in her throat.

'It's all right, Lucy. You don't have to do anything.'

'Domi? Lucy? What's wrong?'

Domenico looked down at Chiara and Lucy felt the sudden release of tension as if a band had snapped undone around her chest. She breathed deep, trying to find equilibrium. But Domenico still held her, his touch firm and possessive. A thrill of secret pleasure rippled through her.

'Everything's fine, little one. I've got a surprise for you both.'

The surprise was a trip to the mainland, to a town that climbed steep hills in a fantasy of pastel-washed houses. Lucy wished she had a camera. Everywhere she turned were amazing vistas and intriguing corners.

'Come on, you're so slow.' Chiara tugged her hand.

'I've never seen any place like this.' Lucy lifted her gaze past a tree heavy with huge golden lemons to the view of green hilltops above the town. 'It's beautiful.'

The little girl tilted her head. 'Isn't it pretty where you come from?'

Instantly Lucy had a vision of grey concrete and metal, of bare floors and inmates scarred by life. It seemed like a dream as she stood here in the mellow afternoon sunlight.

'Yes, it is pretty.' She thought of the village where she'd grown up. 'The bluebells grow so thick in spring it's like a carpet in the forest. Our house had roses around the door and the biggest swing you ever saw underneath a huge old tree in the garden.'

Summers had seemed endless then. Like this one. Except it had to end.

She'd have to forget trying to find a bookkeeping job. Instead she'd look for casual waitressing when she got to England. Something that didn't require character references.

'Come on.' Chiara tugged her hand again. 'Domi said we can have a *gelato* in the square.'

Lucy let herself be led back towards the centre of town. Domenico would have finished his errand for Chiara's *nonna*. He'd be waiting. Her heart gave a little jump that reminded her forcibly that it was time to leave for England.

Yet her smile lingered. For this afternoon she'd live in the moment. Surely she could afford to store up memories of one perfect afternoon before she faced the bleak future?

They were passing some shops, Chiara hopping on one leg then the other, when a shout yanked Lucy's head around.

'Look! It's her!'

A thin woman on the other side of the narrow street pointed straight at Lucy and Chiara.

'I *told* you it was her when they walked up the hill, but you didn't believe me. So I went in and got this. See?' She waved a magazine, drawing the attention not only of the man beside her, but of passers-by.

Lucy's heart sank. She took Chiara's hand. 'Come on, sweetie.'

But the woman moved faster, her voice rising.

'It's her I tell you. She's a killer. What's she doing with that girl? Someone should call the police.'

Nausea roiled in Lucy's belly as she forced herself to walk steadily, not break into a sprint. That would only frighten Chiara. Besides, fleeing would only incite the crowd. She remembered how a mob of inmates reacted when they sensed fear in a newcomer.

Skin prickling from the heat of so many avid stares, she tugged Chiara a little faster. Around them were murmurs from a gathering crowd.

The woman with the magazine came close but not close enough to stop their progress. But the malevolent curiosity on her sharp features spelled trouble. For a moment Lucy was tempted to snarl a threat to make her shrink back.

But she couldn't do it. She couldn't bear to regress to that hunted woman she'd been, half-savage with the need to escape, ready to lash out at anyone in her way.

It had only been a few weeks since her release but they'd altered her. She'd lost the dangerous edge that had been her protection in prison. Besides, what sort of example would that set? She squeezed Chiara's hand and kept walking.

'Why doesn't someone stop her?' the woman shrieked. 'She's a murderer. She shouldn't be allowed near an innocent child.'

Out of the corner of her eye, Lucy saw the picture in the magazine she waved like a banner. It was a close-up of Lucy getting into Domenico's limousine. The headline in blood-red said, 'Where Is Sandro's Killer Now?'.

Her heart leapt against her ribcage as fear battered her. The nightmare would never end, would it? Now Chiara was caught in it. She felt the child flinch as the woman screeched. Anger fired deep inside.

She stopped and turned, tugging Chiara protectively behind her.

The woman shrank back apace. 'Don't let her hurt me! Help!' Instantly others surged forward, curious.

'*Signora*—' Lucy dredged up a polite tone '—please don't shout. Can't you see you're frightening my friend? It would be much better for everyone if you didn't.'

The woman gawped, opening then closing her mouth. Then she hissed, 'Listen! She's threatening me.'

'Lucy?' Chiara's voice was unsteady, her eyes huge as Lucy turned to reassure her, stroking her hair and plastering what she hoped was a confident smile on her face. But inside she trembled. This was turning ugly.

'Grab her, someone. Can't you see she shouldn't be with that child?'

There was a murmur from the crowd and Lucy sensed movement towards her. She spun around to confront a sea of faces. Her stomach dived but she drew herself up straight.

'Touch me or my friend and you'll answer to the police.' She kept her tone calm by sheer willpower, her gaze scanning back and forth across the gathering.

The words were loud even over the mutterings of the crowd. And enough to hold them back…for now.

Domenico took in the defiant tilt of Lucy's head and her wide-planted feet, as if she stood ready to fight off an attack. But she couldn't fend them off. Her hands were behind her back, holding Chiara's.

She looked like a lioness defending her young.

A lioness outnumbered by hunters.

Something plunged through his chest, a sharp purging heat like iron hot from the forge. His hands curled into fists so tight they trembled with the force of his rage. He wanted to smash something. Preferably the shrewish face of the woman stirring the crowd.

He strode up behind Lucy.

She must have sensed movement for she swung round, her face pale.

Her eyes widened. She gulped, drawing attention to the tense muscles in her slender throat and the flat line of her mouth. She looked down, murmuring reassurance to Chiara, but not before he'd seen the fear in her eyes. Half an hour ago those eyes had danced with pleasure at the sight of the pretty town and its market stalls.

Naked fury misted his vision.

Domenico stalked the last pace towards her. In one swift movement he scooped up Chiara and cuddled her close. He looped his other arm around Lucy and pulled her to him. She was rigid as a board and he felt tension hum through her, an undercurrent of leashed energy.

'I don't know who you are,' he growled at the harridan in the thick of the crowd, 'but I'll thank you not to frighten my family.'

Beside him Lucy jerked then stilled. He heard her soft gasp and rubbed his palm up her arm. It was covered in goose bumps. *Damn him for leaving them alone!*

'But she's—'

'It doesn't matter who she is, *signora*. But I'll have your name.' His voice was lethal. 'I'll need it for my complaint to the police. For public nuisance and harassment.' He watched the woman wilt. 'Possibly incitement to violence.'

He turned and glared at the gathering, which had already thinned substantially.

'And the names of anyone else involved.'

He turned to Chiara, giving them time to digest that. 'Are you all right, *bella*?'

She nodded. 'But Lucy isn't. She was shaking.'

'It's all right, little one. I'm here now and Lucy will be fine.'

Domenico felt Lucy shudder and held her tighter, wishing he had both arms free to hold her. Wishing he hadn't dispensed with security support today. He turned back to the street. Only a couple of people remained, watching wide-eyed. He heard the woman at the front whispering.

'He's the one in the magazine. The one whose—'

'*Basta!*' He scowled. 'One more word from you and I'm pressing charges.' He gave her a look he reserved for underperforming managers. A moment later, she and her companions had scuttled away.

'Right, girls.' He turned towards the main square, his arms tight around Chiara and Lucy, his tone as reassuring as he could make it over simmering fury. '*Gelato* time. I'm having lemon. How about you?'

CHAPTER TEN

Lucy shoved her spare shoes into her bag. Just as well she didn't have much to pack. She'd be done in no time.

Then what? the little voice in the back of her head piped up. *Back to the town where you almost caused a riot simply walking down the street?*

She'd talk to Domenico—

No, not him.

She'd talk to Rocco. Surely a security expert could suggest how she could get away and lose herself in the crowds of a big city in England. Anonymity was all she asked. She had no hope of ever getting that in Italy. Not with the press hot on her trail.

Unless she gave in and sold her story.

Her stomach cramped at the idea of lowering herself like Sylvia, her stepmother. That betrayal cut deep. How could Sylvia have done it?

Lucy needed the money, now more than ever. But she needed her self-respect too.

She grabbed a shirt and slapped it on top of the shoes, fighting the hot prickle of tears.

What was happening to her? She hadn't cried in years, not till Chiara's accident. Now she wanted to curl up and blub out her self-pity. It was as if her defences had collapsed, leaving her prey to weakness she'd thought she'd conquered years before.

She looked at the winking lights of the mainland.

A few hours ago she'd been *happy*. Happier than she'd believed possible. The day had been glorious, the surroundings spectacular, and she'd basked in Domenico's approval and solicitude. She'd blossomed into a woman she barely recognised, who actually believed good things might come to pass. Who believed Domenico saw beyond the surface to the woman she was at heart, or was before the last years had scarred her.

She dragged a deep breath into constricted lungs.

He'd been kind, caring, fun. She'd enjoyed his company. More, she'd believed he'd enjoyed hers. And though he hadn't kissed her again, she'd felt the weight of it between them, a potent presence. A promise.

But there could never be more between them. She tried to tell herself he was softening her up to convince her to sign his contract. But she rejected the idea.

Why?

Because she'd fallen for him.

Her hands clenched so hard the nails bit crescents into her flesh.

Pathetic, wasn't she? As if he'd ever care for her.

Maybe those years in jail had warped her judgement—made her ready to succumb to the tiniest hint of caring. She was ready for passion and more, for tenderness, because they'd been denied her so long. That had to be the reason. How else could she explain the way she'd fallen for Domenico like a ripe plum?

She was doing the right thing, getting on with life. This time tomorrow she'd be in anonymous London.

'What do you think you're doing?'

His voice slid like a finger of dark arousal down her spine. Lucy trembled and clutched her clothes tight. Her heart pounded so hard it seemed in danger of bursting free.

'Packing.' She didn't turn. This was difficult enough already. Domenico made her weak in too many ways.

Her pulse thundered as she waited for his response. Maybe he'd turn and leave, glad to be rid of her.

When he spoke again he was so close his words

wafted warm air on her neck. She shivered with longing.

'No, you're not.'

Lucy spun round, dropping clothes from nerveless fingers.

'I *beg* your pardon?' She drew herself up. 'Don't tell me what to do.'

But her defiance was hollow. Her heart wasn't in it. Especially when the sight of his arrogant, endearing, brooding features clamped a different sort of pain around her chest.

She yearned for him to pull her into his embrace as he had earlier and convince her that everything would be okay.

Except it wouldn't. Nothing could make this right.

'You're not the sort to run away when things get tough.'

Lucy's eyes widened at the compliment.

Or did he just see her as prison-tough and able to weather anything?

'Watch me!' She turned to her case but he grabbed her upper arm and hauled her round towards him.

Shock froze her. Some part of her brain rehearsed the quick, violent action that would make him break his hold, yet she made no move to free herself.

'You're not a coward.'

He was so close his words caressed her forehead.

Unbidden, rills of pleasure trickled across sensitive nerve endings.

'This isn't just about me. What about Chiara? She got caught up in this.'

'You're using Chiara as an excuse.'

'Excuse?' Her voice rose to a screech as guilt and despair filled her. 'Don't you understand what happened back there?' She waved an arm towards the mainland. 'I've seen what a mob can do. I don't want Chiara or anyone else put in danger because of me.'

Lucy yanked her arm free and marched to the door, gesturing for him to leave. He followed, but only to stand before her, hands on hips and mouth stern.

'Our business isn't finished.'

'*Your* business, not mine!'

Cold washed through her as she realised that was what mattered to him. Signing that contract. Selling her soul and her chance to prove her innocence.

That was all she was. A problem to be sorted.

That was the only reason he'd been so nice to her. Nice enough for her to weave foolish dreams all over again.

Lucy thought she'd dredged the depths of despair but Domenico opened up a whole new chasm of it. She trembled on the brink of a vast void of anguish.

'I'm leaving.' Her words were clipped by welling emotion.

'You're going because you're scared.'

'Scared? Me?'

Her eyes rounded as he reached out one long arm and pushed the door shut with a decisive click.

'Oh, yes,' he purred in a low, menacing tone that made the hairs on her nape rise. 'You.' His face was implacable. Fear rippled through her.

Or was it excitement?

She stared, unable to break his gaze. What she saw unnerved her. Those hooded eyes were dark as a stormy sky, piercing as a dagger to the chest. She tried to fill her lungs and couldn't.

'*I'm* the menace to society, remember? People are scared of *me*.'

The bitter twist to her lips and the wretched, jarring note in her voice tore through Domenico's good intentions.

He pressed forward till she was flush against the wall.

Something wrenched in his gut at her retreat. He read her haunted expression, the jut of her chin and the shadows in her eyes.

Silently he cursed.

He refused to let her retreat into her shell again.

She'd just let him discover the warm, vibrant woman behind the sassy attitude and touch-me-not air.

Briefly he thought of his family responsibility but nothing had the power to pull him back now. What was between Lucy and himself was every bit as important as his reverence for Sandro's memory.

'What have I got to be scared of?' It was pure bravado speaking but he heard the pain beneath. His heart clenched even as anger and anticipation surged.

'This.'

He took her jaw in his left hand, splayed his right on the wall beside her head and kissed her with all the force of his pent up fury and desire.

His senses convulsed in an explosion of pleasure. The sweet scent of her filled him, and her body against his was pure enticement. He swallowed her gasp of shock and heard it turn to a mewl of pleasure that revved his need higher. A shiver rippled through her and she arched against him, tearing away his last coherent thought.

He tasted her on his tongue, tart and sweet, like citrus and sugar syrup. Deeper he delved, needing more. Needing all she had.

The world tilted then righted itself as, with a groan of surrender, Lucy opened her mouth, luring him deep with the flick of her hungry tongue against his.

Instantly heat ignited in his groin. He pressed her to the wall, ravaging her mouth. Days of desperate longing had built need so deep one kiss couldn't satisfy. Domenico swept his hand down her arm and across to the swell of her breast. She stiffened, then desperate fingers threaded his hair, holding him to her as she kissed him with a passion that made his senses swim.

He squeezed her breast, rejoicing as its lush weight fitted his palm. His grip tightened and he wondered dimly if he should ease his hold but Lucy pressed closer, sending the last of his control spiralling into nothingness.

He was burning, fire instead of blood running in his arteries, hunger humming through each nerve and sinew.

Tearing fingers wrenched her shirt undone so he could tug her bra down beneath her breast. Her skin was silk and heat. His hand shook as he toyed with her nipple and heard her gasp of surrender.

He wanted to feast on her breast, lave her nipple and watch her writhe in pleasure. But he didn't have the patience.

One touch had sparked the powder keg of desire he'd guarded so long. Bending his knees, he ground his hips against hers, rejoicing in the friction against the warm centre of her womanhood. Lightning filled the blackness behind his eyelids.

'More!' Lucy gasped against his mouth, her hands almost painful against his scalp as she strained higher against him.

In his arms she grew frantic, her breath coming in little hard pants as she pulled her mouth from his and nuzzled his collar aside to bite the curve between his neck and shoulder.

Domenico shuddered as a bolt of jagged fire transfixed him.

He rocked into her again and she lifted one leg, wrapping it around his thigh as she tried to climb him.

A man could only withstand so much.

Hands at her waist, he hoisted her high, satisfaction rising as she wrapped him in her thighs, locking her ankles hard as if closing a trap.

She had no need to trap him. He was only too eager. He surged, wedging her back against the wall. His skin was too tight to hold the rising tide of need.

Through slitted eyes he saw the flush of arousal on her cheeks, the long line of her throat as she tilted her head back and her pure alabaster breast, tipped a delicate rose pink.

He'd never seen anything so arousing in his life. Or so beautiful. For a heartbeat he stilled, drinking in the sight of her, tenderness vying with pure animal lust at the way she opened herself to him.

Then her hand brushed the straining zip of his trousers and his body's needs banished all else. Between them they fumbled his zip down. Somehow Domenico freed himself of his underwear, not even bothering to wrench his belt undone.

He let his palms slide up the smooth invitation of her thighs, rucking up her skirt as he went. Quickly he reached for her panties, meaning to haul them aside just enough, but he misjudged his grip. They tore and fell, leaving her completely open.

'Lucy.' His voice clogged deep in his throat but she heard because she opened heavy eyes. Her blue gaze was feverish and he couldn't mistake the desire he saw there.

Yes! *This* was what he wanted from her. Total abandonment. His blood sang with triumph.

With a last shred of sanity Domenico reached for his wallet. Was there a condom there? He wasn't into one-night stands but the habits of youth, or of caution were ingrained. Hopefully...

Lucy kissed him hard, her tongue swirling, drawing him towards oblivion as she tightened her legs.

His erection surged, brushing soft hair and even softer skin.

Domenico's pulse drummed a rough staccato beat as they moved together in an age-old rhythm. Arousal escalated to breaking point. One hand at Lucy's breast, he clamped the other around her calf, loving the feel of her encompassing him.

With each slide of their bodies against each other combustible heat rose. She felt so *good*. So perfect against his needy erection. He tilted his hips, enjoying the way she shivered against his shaft. Once more then he'd reach for...

Lucy hoisted herself higher, and on the next slow surge Domenico found himself positioned perfectly. Too perfectly, he realised as he slid a fraction into tight, slick pleasure.

He gritted his teeth, moving his hands to her hips, ready to withdraw and keep them safe. All he had to do was summon the willpower to withstand temptation. It would only be for a moment and then—

Lucy moved against him again, but this time it was a jerky rock of the hips. Her legs clamped tight as a hoarse gasp of shock filled his ears. She shuddered around him. Her body convulsed and Domenico felt her muscles ripple, urging him on. His eyes snapped open and he caught her gaze as she came apart, wonder in her eyes.

Need destroyed thought. He reacted instinctively, thrusting deep. For a teetering moment her body resisted, impossibly tight. So tight there could be only one reason for it. One that blew everything he'd heard about her out of the water. Stunned, he grappled to make sense of it.

Then coherent thought was obliterated as, with a sudden rush he was there at the heart of her, deep enough to feel the last of her shudders against his sensitive flesh.

The sensations were too much, especially with Lucy abandoned and delicious around him. With a cry of triumph he arched high and hard, pumping into her welcoming warmth.

Behind his closed eyes stars and planets whirled, whole constellations and galaxies burst into life and showered light in a dazzling, mind-blowing display. The ecstasy of release was so intense he wondered if he'd survive.

Through it all he felt Lucy's ragged breath on his face, her hands clutching as if she'd never release him.

When Lucy came to she was lying on the wide bed, under a sheet. She had no recollection of

Domenico crossing the room and stripping the sheet back. She'd been dazed and disoriented by that cataclysmic orgasm. Remembering made her shiver, reawakening muscles she hadn't realised she possessed.

'Cold?' Domenico's voice rumbled from the other side of the bed.

She smiled slowly. Did she have the energy to speak?

'Lucy? Are you okay?' The strain in Domenico's voice puzzled her.

'Never better.' Her words slurred as if she'd been drinking. She felt marvellous. Wonderful. She sank into the feather pillow. This was utter bliss. Only one thing was missing. 'Hold me? Please?'

Silence.

'Domenico?'

'You should rest.'

Something in his voice made her drag her eyes open.

He stood on the far side of the bed, fully dressed, the picture of urbane sophistication but for the frown creasing his brow.

Gone was the out-of-control lover. This man didn't have so much as a hair out of place.

For the first time Lucy realised she was naked beneath the sheet. She vaguely recalled her buttons scattering as he'd tugged her shirt open. Her panties were history, a torn scrap on the floor somewhere. But the rest of her clothes? How could she not have noticed him undressing her?

Uneasily she shifted and felt moisture between her legs. Fire scorched her cheeks. She was wet from Domenico. Her belly clenched at the memory of him pumping into her. The power and stark beauty of what they'd shared overwhelmed her.

Looking at his closed face now, she saw Domenico didn't share her joy. He looked as if he'd just made the worst mistake of his life.

In a rush all her pleasure bled away.

'Good idea,' she murmured through frozen vocal cords. 'I think I'll rest.' She rolled away from him, wincing as tender muscles protested.

'Lucy?' His voice came closer. She shut her eyes. She'd never felt more vulnerable.

'Go away. I don't want to talk.'

The bed sank as he sat beside her, making her roll forwards. Putting out an arm to steady herself, she touched solid muscle beneath his cotton shirt. Instantly she dragged her hand back as if stung. She sucked in a shocked breath as skittering awareness filled her. How could that be when she was completely spent after that no-holds-barred loving?

Sex, she reminded herself. Domenico would call it sex. She refused to consider what she'd call it.

She thrust to the back of her mind the feelings she had for him. The ones that grew stronger daily. The ones that had burst into full bloom when he'd called her his family and hugged her in front of that crowd. He'd acted like a man who'd defend her no matter what it cost.

That one act had shattered the last of her fragile defences.

Her mouth trembled as she acknowledged how much he meant to her. How much his good opinion mattered.

This had nothing to do with her years of sexual abstinence and everything to do with Domenico the man.

'Lucy?' A light touch on her forehead stilled her heart. 'I'm sorry.'

'Sorry?' Her eyes popped open.

'What I did just then...'

'What *we* did.' That was the magic of it.

'I was stupid and selfish.'

'What?' She'd lost track of their conversation.

He leaned close and Lucy inhaled the addictive scent of him, layered with something warm and spicy. The scent of sex, she realised.

'I didn't use a condom.' His glittering eyes held

hers as she processed what he said. 'There's no excuse for what I did. But believe me, it wasn't deliberate.'

How could she not have noticed? Not even spared a thought for her safety?

Biting her lip, she sat up, dragging the sheet with her. She thought she'd matured—no longer the naïve girl who'd made the mistake of letting a predatory male into her room. She'd prided herself on her ability to protect herself. Yet she'd had unprotected sex.

'If it's any help, I can tell you I have no infectious diseases.'

She nodded, avoiding his eyes. After what they'd shared it was stupid to feel embarrassed but she was. 'Me too.'

But that left the risk of pregnancy.

Her heart crashed against her ribs. Pregnant with Domenico's baby?

The complications would be enormous. The divided loyalties, the sheer impossibility of it. And yet… Lucy pressed her palm to her stomach. Was it even possible?

Wonder filled her and a niggling sensation that felt like hope.

She'd always wanted children. Nothing had changed that, not even her stint in prison. If anything, that had consolidated her need for a family of her own now her dad was gone.

'You're not on the Pill, are you?'

The hope on his face soured her pleasure. 'No. Surprisingly, I wasn't planning on sex with the first man I met when I left prison.'

Except it was more than sex. It was liking, caring, and something she didn't want to name.

'If there's a baby—'

'Yes?' She felt herself freeze. Yet who could blame him for not wanting her to carry his child? Her heart dipped as she braced herself.

'If there's a baby you won't be alone.'

Her head jerked up and his silvery gaze snared her.

Did he have any idea how much his words meant? Imagine the scandal if she of all people bore his child! She'd half expected him to talk about a termination, not to reassure her.

She opened her mouth then found she couldn't speak. She nodded, dazzled by the warmth his words evoked. For the first time in ages she wasn't alone.

'I didn't hurt you?' His words were abrupt, scattering her thoughts.

Hurt her? He had to be kidding.

'I'm no china doll, you know.'

For a fleeting instant she thought she saw a smile, a masculine smirk of satisfaction quiver on his lips then disappear. She must have imagined it. When she reached out to touch him he shot to his feet as if scalded.

Lucy frowned, watching him pace across the room. He looked out of the window.

'But you were a virgin.' He ploughed his hands through his crisp dark hair. In a man so controlled it was a sign of major turmoil.

A presentiment of fear scudded through her.

Ridiculous! What was there to fear?

Yet why make such a big deal about her inexperience? It hadn't stopped them. She'd wanted him and he'd wanted her and the result had been glorious.

'It doesn't matter, Domenico. Really.'

Her words made no difference. He held himself ramrod stiff, tension in every line of his body.

'It matters.' His tone was harsh.

He swung round, his expression shuttered, no sign of warmth. His eyes were steely, devoid of the connection she'd imagined there.

'I…' Her words trailed off as realisation smashed into her in a sickening blow. She pressed a hand to her belly. Her heart nosedived as her last meal surged upwards.

It couldn't be true. It couldn't!

She jack-knifed out of bed, yanking the sheet around her with shaking hands.

'Why does it matter, Domenico?' Her voice was a scratch of sound, barely audible over her pounding heart.

In vain she waited for him to assure her it didn't. That he was just concerned he hadn't hurt her.

He said nothing.

The shaking in her legs worsened.

She couldn't drag her eyes from his. Domenico's expression was impenetrable. He didn't want her reading his thoughts.

There could only be one reason for that. One reason why the knowledge of her virginity turned him to stone.

Her blood ran cold.

'You utter bastard!' She heaved in a shuddering breath. Only sheer willpower kept her on her feet. 'You wanted proof, didn't you? Proof that I was telling you the truth?' She pulled herself up as straight as she could despite the cramping pain in her stomach.

'That's what this was about! You couldn't let me leave without knowing once and for all if I lied when I said I wasn't your brother's lover or killer.' She drew a breath so sharp it sliced straight through her ribs. 'When I claimed in court to be a virgin.'

Lucy marched across the room on stiff legs, kicking aside the dragging sheet. He stood still as a graven image.

'You had sex with me to find out if I was innocent or guilty! Didn't you?'

She raised her hand and smacked him across the cheek with such force her hand smarted and her arm ached. But it was nothing to the raw, bleeding anguish of her lacerated heart.

CHAPTER ELEVEN

HE DESERVED THAT slap, and more.

Not because he'd had sex with Lucy as some test, but because of the hurt ravaging her features.

He'd known she was stretched to breaking point by what life had thrown at her. She'd confounded the odds and stayed strong despite everything. But he'd seen behind the bravado to the woman who'd faced down disenchantment, betrayal, injustice and pain. The woman who bled inside but would rather die than show it.

Her prickly defensiveness hid a vulnerability that had first intrigued but latterly worried him.

Now he'd added to her pain.

Because he couldn't keep his trousers zipped!

She spun around, the sheet flouncing as she made to stalk away.

His hand snapped out and imprisoned her wrist, jerking her to a stop.

'Let me go. Now!' She had her back to him but Domenico knew she spoke through gritted teeth.

'Not yet. Not till you've heard me out.'

'Heard you explain why it was necessary to get naked with me?' A shudder racked her. 'Oh, that's right. You didn't get naked, did you?' Her voice dripped sarcasm. 'That would be taking it too far, wouldn't it? Why go to so much effort when all you had to do was—'

'Basta!'

She whipped round to face him, her eyes burning like embers, her colour high. 'No! That's *not* enough. You can't silence me.'

'Not even to hear what I have to say?' God help him, but seeing her so passionate, so vibrant, he wanted her again. More urgently than before. Heat drenched him and his body hardened.

He wanted to smother her anger and her protests with his mouth, strip away that damned sheet and take her again and again till she was boneless and didn't have the strength to snark at him.

He wanted to conquer her even as he revelled in her strength and defiance.

Ma che cavolo! What she did to him! What had happened to his ordered, structured life, where sex was simple, satisfying and civilised?

He stepped in and saw her eyes widen. Something other than fury flickered in those blue depths. Disappointment? Pain?

His urgency deflated to manageable levels.

'I didn't have sex with you to check if you'd slept with Sandro.'

'As if I'd believe that now. You heard me say in court I wasn't your brother's lover. If you'd *believed* me it wouldn't have been a shock to you.'

Domenico swallowed. 'It's not that simple.'

'Not simple?' Her voice rose. 'Either you believed me or you didn't.'

He shook his head, for the first time he could remember, floundering.

How did he explain he'd compartmentalised his thoughts—separating his strengthening belief in Lucy's innocence from the harsh fact of Sandro's death? In his heart he'd been convinced Lucy wasn't the woman they'd all believed. Yet he hadn't followed through to formulate the alternative in his mind. He'd been too busy reacting to her to think logically. He'd been too addled by lust and all the other wild emotions she dragged from him.

And too horrified at what he'd have to confront if she *was* innocent—the enormity of how he'd failed her.

'I knew you weren't the woman we'd thought. I knew you weren't totally guilty.'

'Totally guilty.' Her voice was flat. 'That's nice. So I was just a little guilty. Which bit? Maybe I didn't kill Sandro but slept with him for money? Is that what you thought?'

'No! Don't talk like that.' The idea of her and Sandro together had eaten like acid in his belly for too long. Even now when he knew the truth, Domenico couldn't stomach the idea of her with anyone else.

He might be bigger and stronger than her, he might hold her in an unbreakable grip, but she had him reeling.

'I wasn't thinking! All right?' Tension crackled along his spine, augmented by the hefty dose of guilt weighing his belly. 'I wasn't planning to prove anything except how good we'd be together. Satisfied?'

His belligerent tone concealed the fear he'd felt, watching her pack. The thought of her leaving had gutted him, forcing him into actions that weren't planned but driven by his soul-deep instinct not to let her go.

'No, you weren't thinking.' Her face was pale and set. 'If you had been you'd have realised my virginity—' she said the word as if swallowing something nasty '—isn't proof I'm not a killer. The court rejected my offer of a virginity test, remember?'

Fire branded her cheeks and Domenico swallowed hard, remembering the day in court when the relevance of her virginity had been debated back and forth. His stomach dropped. How hard it must have been for an eighteen-year-old innocent, with no one but an impersonal lawyer to support her.

'I'm sorry.' His touch gentled on her wrist. 'That must have been horrific.'

Lucy blinked and stared as if seeing him for the first time. 'It was like being violated while the world watched.'

He felt her skin prickle and smoothed his thumb over her wrist. Guilt soured his tongue and sliced through what was left of his self-respect. How had he got it all so wrong and let her suffer so?

'My inexperience doesn't prove I'm innocent.' She spoke softly now, as if the fire in her belly had died.

Domenico wanted to wrap her in his arms and haul her to him, but one false move would have her lashing out. His cheek still burned from that slap. Not that he cared about being hurt. What he cared about was not hurting her.

Hell of a rotten job he'd done so far.

'For all you know,' she went on, 'I was leading your brother on, like they said, holding out the promise of sex for jewellery and money. Whether I'd actually spread my legs for him doesn't matter.'

'Don't talk like that!' Domenico's voice was hoarse.

'Why not?' She tilted her jaw in challenge. 'It's what I did just now—'

'No. It's not.' She *couldn't* reduce what they'd shared to something so crude. It had been wild and out-of-control, but it had been anything but casual sex. It had been... Dammit, he didn't understand what it was, but he knew it was *something*.

Domenico grabbed her other hand, regardless of the sheet slithering to the floor between them.

Fifteen minutes ago he'd been unable to tear his gaze from her luscious naked form. Now, though his predictable body stirred, his gaze meshed with hers. She looked back with a hauteur that chilled him to the marrow. She was so furious he wondered if she even noticed the loss of the sheet.

He threaded his fingers through hers, entwining them together. 'What just happened wasn't like that.'

'What was it like then?' Her fine brows arched. 'When you didn't even believe me?'

'I believed.' Not coherently, not consciously, because he'd put such effort into hiding from what his instincts told him. He'd shied from connecting all the dots. Because if Lucy was innocent she'd suffered all these years because of a mistake and his family's need for justice.

Because he'd let himself be swayed by hurt pride

*into believing the worst when others claimed she'd
seduced Sandro.*

He'd taken the easy route and avoided confronting his doubts head-on. He'd found comfort in his cosy role of righteous brother.

He'd been too comfortable, too long.

Domenico had never thought himself a coward. Now, seeing how he'd wounded her, he knew himself less than the man he'd always believed himself. His stomach churned.

'Liar,' she whispered.

'I knew you weren't the woman the prosecution painted you.' He sounded desperate. 'I knew you were warm and caring, that your instincts are decent, not self-centred. Look at the way you saved Chiara. The way you faced down a mob to protect her rather than leave her and take to your heels.'

She shook her head. 'Not good enough.'

He knew it wasn't. Shame blistered him as he realised it was the best he could do. He should have been sure *sooner.*

He'd wanted to believe she was innocent. He'd wanted to think her fear of Sandro's old bodyguard pointed to him, not her, being responsible for Sandro's death. But Domenico hadn't made that final leap of faith. Even when he'd felt her virginal body welcoming him home the truth hadn't hit. He'd been completely absorbed in the heady pleasure of potent, white-hot sex more intense than anything he'd known. His own pleasure had ruled him.

It was only afterwards, watching her go limp in his arms that the enormity of what he knew about her struck.

It had fallen into place, everything he felt, knew and guessed about her.

Every instinct had been attuned to Lucy since she'd bent at his car door and stared at him in frozen horror. Fear of being disloyal to Sandro had stopped him seeing clearly. Or was he simply used to the world fitting his expectations? Had he grown so used to his rarefied world he couldn't see the truth before his eyes?

Heat seared his face.

Domenico gestured to the wall where the world had shuddered as they came together. 'I wasn't thinking about your virginity.' Desperation made him speak the unvarnished truth. 'All I could think about was being inside you, filling you till you screamed my name as you came. Filling you till I finally found my own release.' His lungs hurt as he dragged in air. 'Do you *know* how I've hungered for you?'

Her eyes widened as if his words shocked her. A trickle of heat circled in his belly at the idea of shocking her some more, with actions this time, not words.

It was strange how innocent she was in some ways while she was so tough and worldly in others.

'I didn't have some grand plan to seduce you.' He held her gaze, wondering if he had any hope of convincing her. 'It's you who's been seducing me all along.'

'I have not!' She jerked back in his hold. 'You make it sound like I connived—'

'You didn't have to. All you had to do was be yourself.' That was what had hooked him from the start. Her fascinating, richly layered character. Her strength and fiery independence and her warm-hearted generosity, especially with Chiara. Her courage, her pleasure in simple delights, her straight-down-the-line honesty. She was so uncompromising in her truthfulness that even now he found her a challenge. How had he ever believed her deceitful?

Because he'd wanted someone to suffer for Sandro's death.

Because in his grief and rage he'd been too ready to accept the image painted by the prosecution.

Because he'd been jealous of his brother.

'You're like those lawyers, making out I—'

Domenico tugged her to him so her naked body

pressed against his. His senses jangled into over-drive.

Yet Lucy apparently felt none of the seductive friction between them. She held herself proud as a princess.

He fought to keep his mind on what mattered. 'What happened had nothing to do with the trial.' He searched her troubled gaze, frustration filling him when he couldn't read her thoughts. 'You have to believe me.'

'I don't have to do anything.'

That was the hell of it.

He had no right to expect anything, especially after what had been done to her in the name of justice. Yet he wanted her, still, again, more than before.

Any minute now she could wash her hands of him and leave. Who would blame her?

He gathered her closer, one hand shackling her wrist and the other encircling her bare back. Heroically he strove to ignore the silken invitation of her nakedness. He was torn between so many conflicting emotions.

'I know you didn't kill Sandro, Lucy.'

He felt the almighty tremor race through her at his words, saw her eyes pop wide as she stared up at him.

'You can't know it.' She shook her head emphatically, distrust in her gaze. 'You have no new proof. Nothing. I told you, the fact that I didn't sleep with Sandro—'

'I understand.' He released her hand and lifted his fingers to her cheek, hesitating a moment before sliding his fingers into her hair. 'Technically it doesn't prove your innocence.'

But he knew in his gut, with every instinct, that she was innocent. Finding that she was a virgin had simply been the shock that made the pieces fit together.

No wonder he'd been plagued by doubts. Nothing about the woman he'd come to know fitted with the woman the prosecution had portrayed in court.

'I won't ask you to forgive me for doubting you so long.' That would be asking too much. 'But you must know I'm sorry for what happened. More sorry than I can say.'

He recalled how she'd watched him in court, waiting for him to go to her. And he, blind fool, had been so wrapped up in prejudice and hurt pride, he'd spurned her instead of listening to his instincts. Even though an extramarital affair was out of character for Sandro, Domenico had believed it because Lucy had knocked him off his feet and he was scared by the conflicting emotions she aroused.

In his neat world, no woman had the power to un-
settle him.

'And I'm going to prove you didn't kill Sandro.'
That wouldn't erase the last five years, but he owed
her.

He read something that might have been wonder
in her face. Hope dawned on her fine features. Her
lips trembled and she swallowed hard. His throat
dried as he saw her struggle with emotion.

How alone she'd been, with no one on her side.
She deserved better.

Then she blinked and her mask of indifference
dropped into place. The one she used to keep the
world, and him, at bay. The one he was beginning
to hate. He wanted to strip it away and smash it, so
she couldn't hide from him any longer.

His pulse drummed at the intensity of what he
felt.

He was so caught up in his thoughts he didn't
move to stop her when she backed away, scooping
up the sheet and wrapping it tight around her.

He tried not to notice the way the cotton moulded
her ripe breasts and pebbled nipples. Impossibly,
the flimsy cover only made him more aware of her
delectable body beneath.

'Why would you try to prove my innocence?'

Suspicion filled her voice and he was struck anew by how hard it was for her to trust.

'Because of the wrong done you.' Wasn't it obvious?

'That's not your problem.'

Domenico frowned. Didn't she want his help?

It didn't matter; she was getting it whether her pride revolted at the idea or not.

'I should have questioned earlier. Instead an injustice has been done in the name of my family. To ignore that would be cowardly. Not to act would bring shame on my family and me. I owe you.'

Lucy looked up into that dark, proud face, honed by a centuries-old aristocratic gene pool and the assurance born of success, wealth and privilege.

Despite the intimacies they'd just shared—maybe because of them, with him smartly dressed and her naked beneath a sheet—she felt the yawning chasm between them more than ever.

He spoke of family honour as if that was all that mattered.

Her heart dived. She'd thought for a moment his concern was for *her*. Instead it was for the precious Volpe name. She knew how devoted he was to it after he'd gone to such lengths to preserve it. He'd even brought her from prison to his home.

He hadn't done it for her. It was for his family.

She'd been right. He'd had sex. He hadn't made love.

'I'm not interested in preserving your family's honour.'

His eyes narrowed to glittering slits. 'This is about clearing *your* name. Rehabilitating you in the eyes of the world.'

Despite all logic, hope leapt in her chest. But only for an instant.

'That's something even you can't do.' If she'd had evidence to prove her innocence she'd have used it.

His head reared back as he folded his arms over his broad chest, the epitome of male confidence. 'Watch me.'

He spoke with the assurance of a man who took on disastrous financial markets and won. Who'd built an empire against all known trends. Who succeeded where so many others crashed and burned. A man who never failed.

But he'd learn as she had. The task was impossible. She'd hoped to clear her name but she'd accepted now she couldn't.

'Good luck with that, Domenico. But I don't care to stay around and watch you fail.'

Fire sizzled in those slitted eyes. Anger or challenge?

He paced towards her and to her horror Lucy found herself retreating.

'One way or another we're going to reintroduce you to society. You will *not* be on the run from troublemakers like that harridan this afternoon.' She opened her mouth to protest but he kept right on talking. 'If it's humanly possible, I'll find a way to overturn the court's ruling.'

Lucy wrapped her arms around herself, torn between wanting to believe he meant it and worry that he did. She didn't have the strength to keep fighting, much less go through another bout with the criminal justice system. The thought of it made her flesh crawl.

'You're not going anywhere, Lucy, till we've made this right.'

That's what he was good at, wasn't it? Fixing things, overcoming obstacles. Look at the way he'd risen to the challenge of keeping her from selling her story.

Only now he saw it as family duty to rectify the wrong done in their name. He'd do what he could to put things right because honour demanded it and then... What?

He'd walk away.

Better to make the break now, while she could. For no matter how she tried to deny it, her emotions were engaged. What she felt for Domenico petrified her.

'You haven't thought this through.' She wrapped the sheet more securely and walked to the bed where her case now rested on the floor. She lifted it onto the bed. 'Any scheme to "rehabilitate" me will attract press attention. The media circus would get worse and your family privacy would be a thing of the past.'

Guilt or no guilt, that would make him leave her alone. In a contest between family and the woman he'd lusted for briefly, family would win every time.

She bit her lip and reached for a shirt to put in the case. To her horror, her hand shook visibly.

A long arm reached around her and took the shirt from her grasp. He stood so close behind her she felt the blazing heat of his body warm her. Lucy stiffened.

'I don't care.' His words brushed her nape and shivered around her. 'I have to do this, Lucy. Don't you understand? Everything has changed.'

She stood transfixed as his words sank in.

How she wanted them to be true.

His hand wrapped around hers but this time his touch was infinitely gentle. Slowly he turned her towards him. For the life of her, Lucy couldn't resist.

When he demanded, she could stand up to him. But his tenderness? It undid her.

'Nothing has changed. Don't you see?' Her chest was too tight as she looked into eyes the colour of soft mist in the morning. 'I've lived with this. I *know*.'

'*Cara*.' The simple endearment stole her breath, or maybe it was the way he looked at her. As if he saw only *her*, not some debt of honour. 'You have to trust me, at least for a little longer.'

'I—' His thumb brushed her bottom lip as he cradled her jaw, the heat of his hand pure comfort after the inner chill she'd battled so long. It made her forget that she no longer knew how to trust.

'Let me help you, Lucy. Let me try to make amends.' He leaned forward till his mouth almost brushed her cheek. Her eyelids grew heavy as that riot of sensations started up inside. 'Please?'

The rich timbre of his voice detonated explosions of delight across her senses. Her head swam.

Domenico leaned closer, his lips brushing hers with a tenderness that almost undid her. Lucy's heart pounded and she jerked her head back.

'Don't do that!' If only she sounded as if she meant it. 'I don't want you to kiss me.' She shoved her palm against his chest but that only brought her in contact with his muscled heat.

'Liar,' he whispered in her ear, sending sensual pleasure spiralling through her. His mouth grazed her cheek, then his lips were at the corner of her mouth.

'I said no!' With a supreme effort she pulled out of his hold to stand, panting with exertion as if she'd run a marathon. That was how strong the sensual current of awareness she fought. 'You don't have to seduce me, remember? You already know all about my sexual experience. You've got nothing else to prove.'

Meeting his eyes was one of the most difficult things she'd done. Lucy felt stripped bare, the memory of her passion, her complete sexual abandon, glaringly proclaiming her weakness for him.

'You have no idea, do you, *cara*?' He shook his head, his mouth a grim line. 'This isn't about proving anything, except how much I want you. How perfect we are together.'

In a sudden, shocking movement, he tugged his shirt free of his trousers, pulling it over his head and away.

Lucy's throat narrowed and the air hissed from her lungs as she surveyed his chest—a dusting of dark hair over golden skin, a torso full of the fascinating dips and bulges that proclaimed his body's muscled power.

'I want you, Lucy. The same way you want me.'
He kicked off his shoes and bent to strip away his
socks before she could formulate a reply.

She stepped back, horrified, as her resistance
crumbled at those simple words. Was that all it
took to make her putty in his hands? The backs of
her legs hit the mattress. Dazed, she thought of escape, but couldn't summon the energy to try.

Or maybe she didn't want to. The memory of ecstasy held her still.

As she watched, he made short work of his belt
and zip, only pausing to retrieve his wallet before
letting his clothes drop to the floor.

She'd seen him in bathers, with water plastering
the fabric to his strong thighs and taut backside. But
she'd never seen him naked. She wanted to reach
out and trace the lines of his body. She wanted…

Domenico let the wallet drop and tossed a foil
packet onto the bedside table. The sight of it made
her skin prickle and heat swirl deep in her womb.
He swept her bag off the bed and, dazed, she saw
her belongings scatter across the floor.

She couldn't believe she stood, unmoving, waiting for his touch.

Except it was what she wanted—Domenico's passion and warmth. She craved the sense of being
linked not just bodily but soul to soul. It almost

didn't matter that it was an illusion. What he did to her was magic and, despite every argument common sense mustered, she couldn't turn her back on it. On him.

Not yet.

'Carissima.'

He took her in his arms as if she were fragile gossamer. Only the glitter in his eyes and the tremor in his touch revealed how hard it was for him to take his time.

Yet take his time he did, learning her body with a thoroughness that made her squirm in ecstasy and increasing desperation. Along the way she discovered some of his weaknesses. When she trailed her fingertips across his hip and down to his groin he sucked in his breath. When she nipped at his throat he groaned aloud and when she took his shaft in her hand he rolled her onto her back and pinioned her with the full weight of his body. She revelled in the sense of his powerful frame blanketing her.

'Do that again and this will be over in seconds,' he growled.

'Don't treat me like a piece of porcelain.' She stared up into stormy eyes, loving that she'd made him lose his cool. 'I want you. Now.'

Domenico's sudden feral smile should have scared

her. Instead, fire licked her veins. She wriggled, her thighs opening wider, and he sank onto her.

His smile faded and her breath hitched.

What followed was testament to Domenico's iron control and sexual prowess. He brought her to not one but several peaks of ecstasy, till she thought she'd die from the force of the pleasure pounding through her.

Then at last he joined her, reaching his climax just as Lucy's world shattered in a whirling kaleidoscope of fractured colours and pleasure-drenched senses that surely would never recover from the onslaught.

For the longest time they clung together, hearts pounding in sync, gasps mingling and bodies so entwined it seemed they were one entity.

Lucy never wanted it to end. She never wanted to let him go.

She squeezed her eyes shut, imprinting the moment on her memory, knowing this couldn't last.

Finally, mumbling about being too heavy, Domenico rolled away. Instantly cold invaded her body. Even when he hauled her close, his arm around her and her head pressed to his thundering heart, she couldn't recapture that moment of perfect communion.

Lucy reminded herself that sexual pleasure was fleeting. The sense of let-down was natural.

But it was more than that.

She listened to Domenico's breathing slow, felt his heart beneath her cheek return to its normal beat. But even when her pulse slowed too, she felt anything but normal.

That was what petrified her.

She'd lost part of herself to Domenico Volpe. A part she could never get back.

CHAPTER TWELVE

'I STILL THINK this is a huge mistake.' Lucy stood in the vast dressing room of Domenico's master suite in the Roman palazzo, staring at the plastic-draped clothes lining one wall.

Exquisite designer clothes. All for her.

She clasped her hands as nerves snaked through her. This wasn't just a mistake, it was looming catastrophe.

'How could you even *think* this would help?'

'Because attack is the best form of defence, didn't you know?' Domenico's voice came from the adjoining bathroom. She gritted her teeth at his casual tone.

Didn't he know how much she risked, being seen in public with him?

Of course he did. When this backfired it would smear his name as much as hers. The thought made bile churn and she pressed her hand to her stomach.

She had to find calm.

Calm! The last three weeks had been anything but calm.

Lucy fought down the pleasure that always hovered at the memory of Domenico's loving. Anyone would think they'd be sated now, worn out by the amount of time they'd spent naked together.

Instead she felt energised. When she was with him she almost believed she could take on the world. Especially as she'd decided to make the most of each precious moment.

This interlude couldn't last. When he'd done his best to clear her name they'd go their separate ways. If she'd learnt anything in scouring the press reports it was that he moved in a world far beyond hers. One that collided with hers only due to the circumstances of Sandro's death.

Domenico favoured elegant brunettes who fitted that world as she never could. Socialites and celebrities who took luxury as their due.

Lucy had no illusions. She was a novelty, a wrong to be righted. Domenico felt only lust, guilt and a determination to do right. Tellingly, he never spoke of a future for them beyond that.

When he failed, as inevitably he would, he'd turn to some gorgeous woman from his own rarefied world and Lucy would go far away to start again. All she'd have was memories.

Pain seared, banishing her nerves.

Who knew how long she had with Domenico? Tonight could be the beginning of the end.

Lucy tried to tell herself it had been worth it, these weeks of indulgent delight. She'd made her choice and settled for fleeting joy. She was strong and aware of the consequences. She simply chose to enjoy pleasure while it lasted, rather than wallow in self-pity.

Time for that later.

There could be no future for them, even if she did...*care* for Domenico.

Lucy grimaced at the way she avoided even thinking the alternative word.

What choice did she have? Domenico might be a wonderful lover, passionate and heart-stoppingly demanding. He might be single-minded in pursuing proof of her innocence, but that was guilt at work and his obsessive drive to make things right.

He might be tender with her but only in the way a man treated his current temporary lover. He never spoke of *them*, or of the future, only of clearing her name. He felt guilty because he hadn't trusted her all those years ago.

Domenico was a decent man, a good man, despite his arrogant certainty that the world would bow to his will, but there was no chance he could ever love her.

'Still not dressed?'

Lucy whipped around to find him leaning against the doorjamb, resplendent in a dinner jacket, his fresh-shaved jaw pure temptation to a woman who couldn't get enough of him.

She curled her fingers into fists and looked away, ignoring the inevitable jangle of awareness that cascaded through her.

'I still think this is nonsensical. What will it achieve, being seen in Rome with me? Nothing but more scandal.'

'What it will achieve—' he crossed to stand beside her '—is to prove I'm proud to be with you. That the past is the past. That's a first step.' He dragged a finger across the sensitive skin beneath her ear and she shivered.

'But it will do no good, don't you see?' She looked up at him. 'There'll be a rash of stories about me moving from one brother to the other.' She swallowed hard, trying to rid herself of the bitterness on her tongue.

'Ah, but there'll be far more revealed, just you wait and see. Soon things will seem a lot brighter.' He looked suspiciously pleased with himself.

'What do you know? Is there something?' She couldn't help the surge of hope that dawned.

'Soon, *tesoro*. I promise you, soon this will all be over.'

Logic told her there could be no proof unless Bruno confessed. But Bruno Scarlatti had been happy to let her bear his punishment. That wouldn't change.

Besides, Domenico was right. If by some miracle he did prove her innocence all this would be over. Not just the public burden of guilt, but their time together.

He stroked her again, lingering where the neckline of her T-shirt dipped. His eyes turned smoky dark and Lucy's pulse accelerated. One fleeting touch and she wanted so much more!

It was the knowledge of her neediness that gave her strength to step back.

'You don't trust me with your news?'

The sexy smile curving his mouth died. 'It's not that. I need to have it confirmed. It should be soon.' He paused, raking her face as if searching for something. 'But there is *some* definite news. As soon as you're ready we'll go downstairs and you'll hear all about it.'

'Why don't you tell me now? It's my name you're trying to clear, damn it!' She jammed her hands on her hips. She wasn't used to standing back and relying on others. It made her uneasy.

Domenico leaned in, the glint in his eyes pure devilment.

'Because I know, *cara*, that if I don't give you a reason to get changed and come downstairs, we'll have another argument about you accepting my charity.' He waved a hand towards the wardrobe stuffed full of expensive clothes. 'But now you know the only way to discover what I've found out is to do what I want...'

His smile was all arrogant male satisfaction. Exasperation filled her.

Lucy pressed her hand to his dinner jacket, feeling the steady beat of his heart. She let her fingers slide down the lapel, her fingers brushing his shirt. His muscles contracted beneath her touch.

She let a knowing smile play on her lips. The sort of smile she'd learned from *him*. It hid her skittering fear. Fear that she wanted too much from him.

'I wouldn't say it's the only way I could find out.' Her voice dropped to a husky note as she rose on tiptoe and pressed her lips to a point at the corner of his jaw.

He couldn't hide the way his muscles clenched tight, or the slight hitch to his breathing.

'Witch!' He stepped back, putting space between them.

'Coward,' she purred, pleased more than she

should be. Sexually, there was no denying her power over him.

'A wise man knows when to retreat. I'll wait downstairs.' He made for the door then turned, his mouth curling in a piratical smile that turned her knees to jelly. 'But there'll be a reckoning later, *cara*. You can be sure of that.'

Domenico looked up at the sound of heels tapping on the travertine floor. He moved to the door of the drawing room, only to stumble to a halt.

Shock slammed into him. Shock and what felt remarkably like awe.

He knew every inch of Lucy's delectable body, each dip and curve and enticing hollow. Her face was the last thing he saw at night and the first thing he saw in the morning.

And yet she had the power to stun him.

Per la madonna!

A fine sweat broke out on his brow and heat misted his vision.

He thought he'd known, but he'd had no idea!

A vision stalked towards him in killer heels that made her hips sway in an undulating rhythm that took his pulse and tossed it into overdrive. A full-length gown in glittering gold clung like sin. It scooped low from tiny jewelled shoulder straps to skim the upper swell of her high breasts. The skirt accentuated the long, delicious curve of hip and thigh, hugging close before swirling out around her ankles.

Domenico hitched a finger inside his collar to loosen its suddenly constricting pressure.

'Lucy.' The word was a croak of shock. 'You look…' words failed him '…beautiful.'

More than beautiful. She was luminous. Her eyes were bigger than ever, her lips a glistening, tinted promise of pleasure to come.

He wanted to haul her back to bed.

What was he thinking, planning to show her off to the hungry wolves of Roman society? What madness possessed him?

'I told you it was too much.' She gestured to the dress as she stopped before him and he read the doubt in her eyes.

How could she doubt for a moment how fabulous she looked?

But he'd learned the woman behind the bravado was full of surprises. His chest tightened at the lack of confidence her words revealed. Only now was he beginning to understand how imprisonment had scarred her.

His belly hollowed with guilt.

How could he ever make it up to her?

Domenico reached out and took her cold hand, raising it to his lips as he held her gaze. He turned her hand and pressed a kiss to the soft underside of her wrist, then another, and was rewarded by her shiver of pleasure. Colour tinged her cheeks and her eyes turned slumberous.

'You look perfect,' he murmured in her ear. 'The most beautiful woman in Rome.'

And even now she might be carrying his child.

He'd relegated the idea to the back of his mind, but seeing her so beautiful yet vulnerable loosened the guard he placed on his thoughts.

A surge of protectiveness filled him.

He forced himself to step back.

Looking into her stunned face, Domenico had an unsettling feeling he'd strayed out of his depth. He'd never experienced anything like it.

He thought he'd known what he was getting into but at each turn Lucy confounded him. Uneasily he banished the suspicion that he, not she, was the one who needed help.

'Come, there's someone here to see you.' He hooked her hand through his and covered her fingers. 'And remember, I'm with you.'

His hand closed around hers in a gesture of reassurance.

She couldn't drag her gaze from his. For the first

time ever she felt truly beautiful, because of the admiration in his eyes.

Domenico ushered her into the spacious sitting room. Walking in breakneck heels was much easier with his support. She could get used to—

Lucy stumbled mid-step, her hand clawing his arm. Her spine set as she fought a primitive instinct to flee.

How could he have done this to her?

'You remember my sister-in-law, Pia.' His voice was smooth, his manner urbane, as if he hadn't just introduced the woman who'd once screamed abuse at her for killing her husband.

Lucy swayed. Her knees weakened and she feared she'd crumple till Domenico wrapped an arm around her.

His hold was all that kept her upright.

Pia was pale and perfect, from her expertly cut dark hair to her exquisite designer shoes. Huge dark eyes surveyed her as if trying to read her soul. Slowly she crossed the room.

Lucy tried to drag in air. She couldn't breathe. Maybe the oxygen had been sucked from the room by the intensity of Pia's stare.

The other woman raised her hand and Lucy flinched.

It took a lifetime to recognise the gesture. A handshake? From Pia Volpe?

Hysterical laughter rose and Lucy bit her lip to stop it bursting out. She shook her head in disbelief.

'You won't shake my hand?' The other woman's face was tight as she shot a look at Domenico. 'I told you, didn't I?'

'Don't be hasty, Pia. Lucy's surprised. She didn't know you were here.'

Because if she'd known she'd never have agreed to come!

Lucy couldn't look away from the face of the woman before her. 'What's going on?' Her words were a rough whisper but at least her larynx worked.

'Come and sit down.' He urged them towards a group of leather sofas. 'There's no need for formality.'

Again that inappropriate gurgle of laughter threatened. He thought they could be casual? She and the woman who blamed her for her husband's death?

Yet she found her legs moving stiffly. A moment later she plopped onto a sofa as her knees gave way. Domenico held her, his body crammed close. If she had the energy she'd elbow him away, but she was hollow with shock.

Pia subsided gracefully into an armchair. She didn't look happy.

'Pia, perhaps you'd explain why you're here?' Domenico's voice was smooth but held a note of steel.

Lucy watched Pia shift and realised it hadn't been her idea to come here.

What was going on?

'I came to…' The brunette darted a look at Domenico then turned to Lucy. Her fingers went to her throat in a nervous gesture. 'To apologise.'

Lucy's breath stopped but her heart pounded on. She opened her mouth to speak but nothing came out.

Pia crossed her legs then uncrossed them, clearly ill at ease.

'I don't understand,' Lucy croaked.

'Domenico told me what he'd found out.'

Lucy jerked in shock, her head swinging round to Domenico. He *couldn't* have told her, could he? Fire scorched her face at the idea of him informing Pia she'd been a virgin.

As if reading her thoughts he shook his head. 'Not that,' he whispered. His hand closed on hers but she shook it off.

'He explained there was new evidence,' the other woman went on, 'about Bruno being the guilty one.'

Lucy darted a look at Domenico but his face was inscrutable.

'I never liked him, you know,' Pia said. 'He was always a bit too smooth. But I never thought…' She shook her head. 'You must believe me, Signorina

Knight. I didn't know he lied. All I knew was Sandro was in your room, with you cradling his head, and he was dead.' She sobbed and lifted a handkerchief to her eyes.

'It's all right, Pia. Lucy understands you didn't know the truth.' Domenico's hand touched Lucy's again and this time she was too distracted to move it.

'Of course,' she said, trying to digest this news. *What new evidence?*

'You understand?' Pia looked up through tear-glazed eyes.

Lucy nodded. 'I didn't know what Bruno was really like either. If I had I'd never have let him into my room.' She shuddered, thinking how gullible she'd been.

Domenico squeezed her shoulders and she had no desire to shake him off.

Pia's hand went again to her throat. 'It was a shock when Domenico told me the truth.' Her mouth curled in a trembling smile as she looked at her brother-in-law. 'You gave Sandro back to me with your news. You have no idea what that means after all this time.'

'It took me too long.' Domenico's voice was grim. 'I should have thought of it years before.'

Lucy looked from one to the other, curiosity mounting. 'Thought of what?'

The other woman turned to her. 'My jewellery, of course.' Her eyes widened. 'Domenico, you didn't tell her?'

'No one has told me anything.' Frustration rose. Everyone knew more than her!

'I thought Lucy would appreciate hearing it from you,' he said.

Lucy bit down a demand for someone, anyone, to tell her what was going on.

'Domenico found the artisan who made my jewellery.' Pia extended her arm. On her wrist was a bracelet of enamelled flowers, exquisitely executed and interspersed with lustrous pearls.

Lucy leaned forward, identifying primroses and forget-me-nots in a design she'd never expected to see again. Her stomach clamped down as icy fingers danced on her spine. Nausea rose and she breathed hard through her mouth, forcing it down.

Abruptly she sat back, shutting her eyes in an effort to regain control.

When she opened them she saw Pia's hand caressing the matching necklace at her throat. Lucy had been so preoccupied she hadn't recognised it.

'That was the necklace they found in my room.' Lucy's voice was hoarse. Stupid to be so affected but it brought back that night in too-vivid detail. More, it evoked memories of how it had been used against her in the trial. 'I didn't know there was a bracelet too.'

'Nor did I,' Pia said, smiling as she looked at her brother-in-law.

Lucy turned in his hold. Domenico's eyes were fixed on her with an intensity that banished the cold prickling her backbone. 'You knew there was a bracelet?' Why was that important? She still didn't see.

'No, I just tried to track down the maker. I was desperate for any leads that might give me a better picture of what happened back then.' His hand tightened on hers.

Her heart dipped. He'd tracked the maker down because he'd sought the impossible—something to prove she wasn't a killer.

'The police were only interested in the fact you had the necklace, not where it was made.'

'Because everyone assumed he'd bought it for me.' Lucy shivered, remembering how the prosecution had made so much about the match between the enamelled flowers and the colour of her eyes. Plus the fact that, beautiful as the piece was, it was nothing like the glittering emeralds and rubies Sandro had previously given his wife. The implication was that he'd got something expensive for his new lover, but nothing to rival the grandeur of the jewels he'd bought his wife.

'But they were wrong. See?' Pia undid the bracelet and held it out.

Lucy couldn't bring herself to touch it. Instead Domenico took it and laid it across his broad palm, revealing the engraved lettering on the back: *To my beloved Pia, light of my life. Always, Sandro.*

'I don't understand.' Lucy's head whirled.

Domenico passed the bracelet back.

'Sandro had commissioned a matching set but only had the necklace the night he was killed. According to the maker, when he came to collect them he decided to have the inscription engraved on the bracelet, but he didn't want to wait to give the necklace to Pia. He took it and said he'd be back for the second piece. When he didn't return and the artisan discovered he'd died, he didn't know what to do with the bracelet. He had no idea of its significance to the case. He thought of removing the inscription and selling it on, but was superstitious enough to think it might bring bad luck.'

'Why didn't your brother wait for both pieces?'

'Because of me.' It was Pia who spoke. The glow of happiness dimmed and her features were sharp with pain.

'I wasn't…well.' Her eyes met Lucy's before shifting away. 'I didn't know at the time. It wasn't till after that night, much later, that Domenico arranged for me to get help.' She swallowed and Lucy felt sympathy surge for the other woman's obvious pain.

'I…' Pia paused and dragged in a deep breath. 'I wasn't myself after Taddeo was born. I was…troubled.' She worked the bracelet on her wrist. 'I was so miserable I accused Sandro of not caring for me and of infidelity.'

Guilt-filled eyes rose to meet Lucy's.

Lucy remembered how difficult and moody Pia had been all those years ago. How she hadn't liked it when Lucy could calm little Taddeo so easily, and how she'd jumped to conclusions when she'd found Lucy and her husband talking together. Poor Sandro had been worried about his wife and son, checking with Lucy about his concerns. He'd been torn between placating his wife and getting help for what Lucy thought could be Pia's severe depression.

'At the trial I said things about you and Sandro.' Pia sucked in a shaky breath. 'Things I believed at the time, but things that looking back I realise I didn't *know*.'

Like stating emphatically that Lucy had been

Sandro's lover, saying under oath she'd found them in compromising positions.

'It wasn't till Domenico came to me with his news, and *this*—' she looked at her bracelet '—that I realised what I'd done.' She paused. 'Sandro and I met in spring, you see. For all his money, Sandro courted me with primroses and forget-me-nots. When he ordered this he was trying to remind me of those early days when we were happy. He was bringing the necklace to me that night, not you. It must have fallen from his pocket when he…when he…'

Lucy leaned across and touched the other woman's hand. 'Your husband must have loved you very much. It was there in his face whenever he mentioned you.'

Pia's eyes filled but she smiled. 'I know that now. But at the time I was so unhappy. That's why I said those things—'

'It's all right, truly.' Even at eighteen Lucy had understood enough to realise Pia hadn't deliberately slandered her. She'd been hysterical with grief and misery, falling easily into supporting Bruno's damning evidence that tied so well with her own imaginings. He'd painted Lucy as an immoral opportunist, no doubt feeding Pia's worst fears. 'I'm sure it made no difference to the case.'

'You think so?'

No. Lucy wasn't certain. She'd seen the court moved by the beautiful grieving widow. But pity was stronger now than any desire for revenge. Pia's regret was genuine, as was her joy at rediscovering her husband's love.

Would Lucy ever know love like that? Her heart squeezed.

'I know it,' she murmured.

'Thank you.' Pia took her hand. 'That means a lot.'

A third hand joined theirs. Then Pia's touch dropped away as she sat back in her seat and Domenico's fingers threaded through Lucy's. Warmth spread from his touch. Not the fire of physical desire but something more profound.

Was he congratulating himself on the reconciliation? One step closer to the day he could wash his hands of his obligation to her?

He looked up at the antique clock above the mantelpiece then rose, tugging her to her feet. 'Come on, ladies. It's time we left.'

Pia rose and reached for a gossamer-fine wrap. It was left to Lucy to ask, 'Where are we going?'

'To the opera, then supper.' He tucked her hand into his elbow. 'We have a reservation at Rome's premier restaurant.'

'But the press! They'll see—'

'They will indeed,' he murmured. 'They'll see that far from shunning you, you're our guest. It will prime them for more news to come.'

CHAPTER THIRTEEN

'IT'S NOT AS bad as I expected.'

Lucy's murmured comment made Domenico smile.

He surveyed the ultra modern restaurant that was Rome's latest A-list haunt and thought of the other women he could have brought here. Women who'd toy with the exquisitely prepared food while making the most of the chance to see and be seen. Who'd have spent the day getting ready to come here.

By contrast he'd had to force Lucy into her glamorous new clothes. She shunned the avid gazes sent their way, concentrating on her food with an unfashionable enjoyment that would endear her to the chef.

'I'm glad you think having supper with me isn't too much of a burden.'

Her gaze darted to his face and her lips quirked in the first genuine smile he'd had from her all night. He couldn't believe how good it felt, seeing that. He'd even wondered, for about half a minute, if he'd done the wrong thing, thrusting her into the limelight again.

Earlier at the opera with Pia, Lucy had stood stiffly as they mingled in the foyer, sipping champagne and chatting with the many acquaintances who'd approached them. The three of them had been a magnet for attention. Yet only he, holding Lucy close, knew what it cost her to appear at ease in the glittering crowd. She'd projected a calm, slightly aloof air that fitted the setting perfectly and she'd held her own with a poise that made him proud.

She truly was a remarkable woman.

'If you're fishing for compliments you're out of luck, Signor Volpe.' But her eyes sparkled. 'It's not *you* I was worried about. It was everyone else.'

'You handled them beautifully.'

She laid her spoon down and licked a stray curl of chocolate from her upper lip. Desire twisted in Domenico's belly, sharp and powerful, and he sucked in his breath.

She aroused him so easily. Each time he had her he wanted her again. Every day he needed more, not less.

How long would it take to have his fill?

'*You* handled them beautifully, not me. No one

dared say anything outrageous with you beside me. But they wondered what was going on.'

Domenico spread his hands. 'Of course they wondered. What do we care for that? Tonight is about making it clear the Volpes accept you. That's why Pia came to the opera. If we champion you, who in society will deny you?'

'It's not Roman high society I'm worried about. It's everyone else. The press, for a start.' She reached for her water glass and drank deeply. It was the only outward sign that she wasn't completely at ease.

'Let me take care of the press, Lucy.' Strange how he found himself deliberately using her name so often. As if he got pleasure from its taste on his tongue.

'Don't you see?' She leaned forward, face earnest. 'You can ward them off with your bodyguards. But when I'm on my own it will be different. They'll bay for my blood even more than before.'

Domenico covered her hand. 'It will be all right. You just need to be patient. If all turns out as I intend, soon you won't have to worry about the press.'

The media would have another victim in its sights. There'd be a spike of interest in Lucy as victim, rather than criminal, but eventually it would die down.

Triumph filled him. After weeks of intense work, they were on the brink of success.

This particular success brought a satisfaction greater than any business coup. Because his pleasure in this was *personal*.

It would salve his battered conscience, clearing Lucy's name. The Volpe family would pay its debt by redressing the wrong done her. More specifically, it would be some small recompense for the way he'd rejected her out of hand.

But there was more. He'd been surprised at how tonight's meeting between Pia and Lucy had affected him. How he'd felt both women's pain.

He'd always thought Pia over-emotional and needy. Now he realised her belief in Sandro's betrayal had fed that neediness. She really had loved his brother. Believing Sandro no longer loved her had undermined her fragile self-worth. Now perhaps she could face the world with a little more confidence.

As for Lucy—he watched her watching him from under lowered lashes and his hold tightened possessively. It might have been responsibility, obligation and guilt driving him to clear her name. But he wasn't just acting out of duty.

He felt *good*, knowing Lucy would be in a better place when this was over.

In the past he'd confined his philanthropy to large charitable donations. Maybe in future he'd take a more hands-on role. He'd discovered he enjoyed righting wrongs and seeing justice done.

But there was another, more personal dimension to this—an undercurrent that flowed deeper and stronger than any do-gooder intentions.

Domenico stroked his thumb across Lucy's palm and felt her shiver. Her lips parted. He wanted to kiss her with all the pent up passion he kept in check.

But he preferred privacy for what he had in mind.

He stroked her palm again, this time drawing his finger past her wrist and along her forearm, watching with satisfaction the tiny telltale signs of her pleasure.

'What do you think you're doing?'

He loved the way her voice dropped to that husky note when she was aroused.

'Nothing.'

He looked up and her sultry gaze caught him. His heart thudded and urgency filled him.

'Liar,' she whispered. 'I know your game.'

'Good.' He drew her from her seat. 'Then you won't mind leaving the rest of your dessert.'

She leaned forward so her breath feathered his cheek. 'Not if you're offering something better.' She turned, collected her shimmering evening bag and headed towards the door with a slow, sexy sway that drew every male gaze.

Domenico was torn between appreciation and dog-in-the-manger jealousy that she flaunted herself in front of others.

In mere weeks she'd blossomed from artless innocent to a siren who turned him into a slavering idiot.

She really *was* remarkable.

Eyes glued to her, he summoned a waiter and had the bill put on his account.

He smiled as she slowed to wait for him at the door.

What more could he want from life? He had the anticipation of success, the satisfied glow that came from redressing past wrongs, and the bonus of Lucy in his bed.

Life was excellent.

It was over breakfast that news came.

Lucy was enjoying a platter of summer fruit when she heard Domenico on the phone. She looked up as he entered the room. Their eyes met and, as ever, her skin tingled.

'I see,' Domenico said into the phone, his eyes

dark with secrets. Images of their loving last night surfaced and she felt an unfamiliar blush rise.

Last night had been…phenomenal. She tried to tell herself it was just reaction, having survived the evening without falling in a heap or being accosted as a criminal. But she knew the magic came from far deeper feelings.

The efforts Domenico went to in order to clear her name were amazing. She owed him a debt she could never repay. He'd achieved more in a few short weeks, with his discovery of the jewellery, than the police had. Presumably because they'd been only too ready to accept Bruno's evidence and blame the outsider—her.

More, he was the one who'd cracked open the brittle shell she'd built to separate herself from the world. It was scary being without it, but wonderful too. These last weeks had been crammed with precious pleasures she'd remember all her life.

She looked away from those penetrating grey eyes.

If only she could feel simply gratitude. But she felt far more. Domenico touched her deep inside. He'd changed her for ever.

'When did this happen?' He paused and Lucy's head jerked up at his tone. 'Excellent. You've done well.' A smile split his face and Lucy caught her breath.

Domenico put the phone down and sat, looking smug.

'What is it? What's happened?' Even as she spoke something tempered her impatience, an atavistic fear of upsetting the good life they shared. Tension scrolled down her spine, like a premonition of cold, hard change to come.

'Good news. The best news.'

Yet, unaccountably, Lucy felt that tension eddying deep inside. Slowly she wiped her fingers on a linen napkin.

Domenico raised his eyebrows as if expecting her to burst into speech.

'The police have taken Bruno Scarlatti in for questioning in the light of new evidence. They're reviewing the investigation into Sandro's death.'

Lucy's heart pounded. 'New evidence?'

'Remember Scarlatti had an alibi for the time of Sandro's death? A colleague who claimed to have been with him on the other side of the palazzo?'

'How could I forget?' Lucy clasped her hands together, old bitterness welling.

'That colleague has come forward, saying he'd got the times wrong. He was with Bruno fifteen minutes earlier rather than at the time of the killing, as he said. There was always forensic evidence Bruno had been in the room but only your word for it he'd been there before Sandro died, not just later.'

'The witness admitted to lying?' It seemed too good to be true.

Domenico shrugged. 'He was young. Bruno was his mentor and friend. He thought he was doing him a favour, giving an alibi for a crime he couldn't believe Bruno committed.'

'You know a lot about this.' Lucy felt strangely disconnected from the news, as if it affected someone else.

'Rocco tracked the witness down and filled him in on Bruno's record since then.'

'He's got a record?' That was news.

'A conviction for assault and a string of complaints. Plus dismissal for questionable behaviour.'

Lucy sat back, her mind awhirl at the implications. 'You did all this.' It boggled her mind.

She waited for elation to hit.

'It was nothing. I had the resources to uncover the truth, that's all.'

Lucy shook her head, her heartbeat loud as a drum. 'It's more than anyone else did.'

'But I knew the truth. That made it easier.' He reached out and took her hand. His felt hard and capable. She looked into his eyes and read satisfaction there. The satisfaction of a man who'd solved a puzzle no one else had. The satisfaction of a man who'd achieved justice, no matter how belated. Who'd restored his family honour by redressing the injustice done in their name.

She slid her hand from his grip and laced her fingers together in her lap.

Dazed, she grappled with what he'd told her. She'd be able to reclaim her good name. It was what she'd longed for and fought for all this time.

Yet instead of euphoria, a sense of anticlimax enveloped her. It all seemed too…easy.

'So you threw resources at it and hey presto, the truth is revealed?' She couldn't hide her bitterness. 'If only the police had done that in the first place— really *listened* and investigated thoroughly…' She shook her head, a wave of anger and frustration engulfing her. '*Five years* of my life gone. Five years in hell.'

When Lucy looked up it was to see Domenico's grim expression.

'You're right. It should never have happened like this. Can you forgive me?'

She frowned. 'Forgive you? I'm talking about the way the investigators latched on to Bruno's evidence and didn't want to hear anything against it because he was one of them, ex-police.'

Domenico's mouth tightened. 'If I'd taken time to hear you out instead of assuming your guilt it would have been different.' His shoulders rose and fell in a massive shrug that spoke of regret and pain.

Suddenly she saw him clearly, right to the shadows in his soul. He expected her condemnation.

So it was true, his actions had been driven by guilt all this time. She sucked in a breath, trying to find calm.

Domenico was many things but, she knew now, he wasn't responsible for her conviction. That notion had been a sop to her anger and pride in the dark days when she'd needed it most.

She didn't need it now. She'd held on to anger and cynicism for too long and she didn't like the woman it had made her.

'Don't talk like that.' Her voice was husky. 'You're the man proving my innocence.'

'But too late. I should have—'

'No, Domenico.' She raised her hand. 'It devastated me when you cut me loose but it didn't make a difference to the trial. It hurt.' She faced him squarely, letting him read the truth. 'But that's all. No one could blame you for doubting me in the face of the other evidence.'

For a long moment searching grey eyes held hers. 'You're some woman, Lucy Knight. Thank you.'

She smiled, though her heart wasn't in it.

She told herself this was the beginning of the rest of her life, the beginning she'd wanted so long, but with it came sadness that her dad hadn't survived to see her innocence proven. And welling dismay over what this meant for her and Domenico.

Lucy rubbed her forehead, trying to ease the ache beginning there.

'Lucy? What is it? Are you all right?'

She looked down at the luscious fruit on her plate and her stomach roiled.

'Of course. I'm just…stunned. It's taking a while to process.'

Could she be pregnant? Was that what made her nauseous and maudlin instead of happy at this brilliant news? The possibility had sat at the back of her mind ever since she'd learned he hadn't used protection that first time.

Joy and fear filled her at the idea of carrying Domenico's child. Despite his assurances, she knew he wouldn't be happy. Innocent she might be, but it had become clear last night, seeing the glitz of the rarefied world he moved in, that she didn't belong. She'd had to call on every ounce of courage to face the calculating gazes of the uber-wealthy and the paparazzi.

She'd even been gauchely enthusiastic about her

first opera when the rest of the audience displayed only polite appreciation. She'd been so obviously an outsider.

'It's okay, Lucy.' His tone was encouraging, kind. 'We achieved what we set out to do. It's all over now.'

Her gaze darted to Domenico's face. In it she read self-satisfaction that, melded onto his superbly sculpted features, gave an air of ingrained superiority.

It's all over.

Hadn't she told herself that what they shared would end soon? She could barely call it a relationship, despite the blinding moments of connection. It was based only on sexual pleasure and convenience. Not once had he spoken of a future beyond 'rehabilitating' her.

As if she was some project instead of a woman with feelings!

Feelings. Oh, she had those in spades.

She tried to dredge up gratitude. Instead a writhing knot of emotion wedged in her chest.

'Thank you,' she said finally. 'Without you, this would never have happened.'

He gestured dismissively. Obviously it had been nothing mobilising vast resources to revisit every aspect of the prosecution case.

Lucy swallowed, not wanting to ask, but needing to know. 'What now, Domenico? What will we do?'

Last night, basking in his closeness, she'd let herself dream what it would be like if he truly cared for her. If he *loved* her.

She snatched in her breath on a desperate gasp. Until now she hadn't used the L word. Coward that she was, she'd avoided even thinking it. But she couldn't pretend any longer. She wanted to be more to Domenico than a project.

She wanted to be in his life permanently. She wanted his laughter, his tenderness, his loving, the way he made her feel precious and special. She wanted to be the woman she'd become on his island, where she'd learned about compassion and trust and...love.

Her stomach dipped at the enormity of what she wanted. She'd gone from total, self-absorbed isolation to knowing she wouldn't be whole without him.

She swallowed hard. She'd fallen in love.

'Now?' His brows drew together.

'Now it's over.'

She waited, longing for him to tell her it would never be over. That he felt this overwhelming sense of belonging with her too, despite the differences between them.

'Nothing more is necessary. The legal experts can take it from here.' He gave her a reassuring smile that did anything but. 'We'll continue the strategy of showing you out and about, accepted by the family and everyone who counts. My security staff will protect you.'

'Of course.' She felt like an inanimate object to be exhibited. Lucy told herself she was unreasonable. It didn't help.

'There'll be a spike in interest once it's clear you're innocent. But in the long run I'm hopeful you can start that new life you want so much.'

His smile was benevolent, like an adult giving a child a long awaited treat.

Except she didn't want it as she once had. Not if it meant leaving Domenico.

But it wasn't her choice to make.

She waited for him to say more. To talk about *them*.

He said nothing.

She read the satisfaction in his eyes and the way he sprawled in his chair. He'd done what he'd set out to do against the odds. Wasn't that his speciality? Succeeding where everyone failed? She'd been one more challenge to a man who revelled in beating the odds.

Lucy's stomach clenched. She wanted to be more.

'Where will you be, Domenico?' She was proud of her even tone when inside she shook like a leaf in a gale.

'Me?' He looked surprised she'd ask. 'I'll stay in Rome for a while to help you through the media attention. You won't have to cope alone.'

No, he'd made it his business to look after her. She told herself she should appreciate it more. She *did* appreciate it, except she felt like a problem to be managed rather than the woman in his life.

Miserably, she reminded herself she'd never really been his woman, just conveniently available.

'And after that?'

He shrugged and reached for his coffee. 'I've got business in New York I've delayed for a couple of weeks.' Delayed because of her.

'And then?' She laced her fingers, willing him to say something, anything about *them*. About coming back to her or taking her with him. 'What about after that?' Even a promise to see her in England would be something.

Domenico frowned, clearly not used to being quizzed.

'It depends on a number of things. Perhaps Germany for a week or two.'

'I see.'

Finally, she did.

This *was* the end.

She'd known it was coming. How could she not, when despite the precious moments of communion, she didn't fit in his world or he in hers?

He'd support her for a week or two more, squiring her and protecting her from the press. And he'd be happy, no doubt, to share his body with her, while he was in town.

After that she was on her own.

Pain stabbed, transfixing her. She breathed slowly through her mouth, willing the searing heat, like a red-hot knife in her midriff, to ease. It didn't, but she couldn't bear to sit here with him surveying her like his latest trophy of success—proof that Domenico Volpe could achieve anything he set his heart on.

When she'd set her heart on—

No! She'd known this couldn't last. She'd resolved to enjoy every minute Domenico gave her and not look back. It was she who'd broken the rules by wanting more.

She prayed she still had the power to hide her feelings from him.

'I never believed you could do it, Domenico.' She let his name roll around her mouth, savouring it one last time. 'Thank you.' She met his gaze, felt that familiar sizzle of heat, then looked at her hands threading together in her lap. She'd have to do better than this if she was to leave with dignity.

'It was my pleasure, Lucy.' The rumble of his voice reminded her of the intimacies they'd shared, not just in bed, but when they'd laughed together, talked, and played with Chiara.

Her shiver of response was the catalyst she needed. She could stay but each day would draw her further into his thrall till she wouldn't have the strength to go. She couldn't wait for the day he decided it was time for her to leave.

Lucy's chair scraped the polished floor as she stood.

'If you'll excuse me I'll go and pack.' She lifted her head and looked at a point just over his shoulder. 'I appreciate your help, but I'd rather not stay in Rome.'

Domenico froze, his coffee halfway to his mouth.

'Prego?' What did she mean, she'd rather not stay?

'It's time I went home. I'm sure you understand.'

The cup rattled as he put it down. Understand? Like hell he did. As for going home, he knew as well as Lucy that she had no home. Her she-wolf of a stepmother had sold Lucy's privacy for a fist-ful of cash.

'No, I don't understand! Perhaps you'd explain.'

How could she be so eager to leave? Indignation stirred and with it male pride. Only hours ago she'd lain in his arms, crying out his name as they found bliss together. Heat stirred, remembering.

She didn't meet his eyes.

Fear prickled the hairs on his nape. He didn't un-derstand it, but he did trust his instincts. Something was wrong. Badly wrong.

'I'm English, Domenico. I want to go to England.'

'You haven't mentioned returning in weeks.'

She shrugged. 'Because it was obvious I'd be hounded by the press. You gave me a place to lie low and I appreciate it.'

Was that all he'd given her? She short-changed them both implying it was.

'I've been in Italy since I left prison. I want to go home.' Her hands twisted. 'Do you realise that, even out of jail, I haven't chosen where I stayed? Not even for a night?'

She complained about the way he protected her? Or did she complain about being with him? Do-menico's mind whirled. It wasn't possible. She'd welcomed him into her bed so eagerly.

'You'd rather I'd left you to the press?' He spoke

through gritted teeth. He told himself he didn't want her gratitude but he sure as hell expected better than this. Anger stirred. 'You know it was for your own good.' Even if at first it had been for his convenience.

She nodded. 'I appreciate all you've done. And the way you came to my aid that day we went ashore. But it's time I stood on my own two feet.'

Domenico's jaw jammed shut. He hated that note of finality in her voice. He wanted to rail at her and tell her she couldn't leave.

But what right had he to stop her?

Only the fact that he wasn't ready to let her go. Not while the passion they shared burned so bright.

Didn't she feel it too?

Or had she simply taken advantage of what he offered, ready to discard him as it suited her?

Domenico's jaw tightened.

Never had a woman dumped him. And never had one left with such little regret. He hated this dark roil of emotions. They made him feel…alarmingly out of control.

He strode around the end of the table, ready to reach out and grab her, only to stop when she faced him with that cold mask of disdain he'd thought she'd ditched for good.

'I'm a free woman now and it's time I acted like one.'

'The press will be after you.' She needed him, couldn't she see that? Something akin to desperation racked him. 'With the case reopened the press will be more eager.'

'I don't care. At least now they won't call me a murderess. They won't stop me getting a job.'

'You want to work?'

Her eyes, like blue stars, met his head-on and the impact rocked him back on his heels.

'Of course I want to work. What choice do I have?' Her expression was dismissive.

'You could always sell your story. They'd pay even higher money for your inside story now you've been in my bed.'

Even as he said it, Domenico regretted the words. She'd goaded him into a quagmire of bitter, unfamiliar emotions, announcing she was leaving. He felt betrayed and he lashed out.

Lucy looked at him as if she'd never seen him before. Her eyes were laser-sharp as they raked him, scraping his flesh raw. Had he really imagined she cared for him?

'Perhaps I will. After all, I didn't sign that gag contract of yours, did I?'

It was a physical blow to the gut, watching her turn back into the ice-hard woman she'd once been.

He wanted to beg her not to do it. But Volpes never begged. Besides, she was beyond listening to him.

'Goodbye, Domenico.' She spun on her foot and left.

CHAPTER FOURTEEN

AUTUMN CAME EARLY to London. Wind gusted down the city street, grabbed Lucy's second-hand jacket and flapped it around her.

The chill didn't bother her. She'd grown used to feeling cold, ever since that day in Rome when Domenico had washed his hands of her.

She tilted her head down and put one weary leg in front of the other. It had been a long day and she needed this short break to regroup before her busy evening shift. Jobs weren't easy to come by, not even casual waitressing jobs, and she had rent due. She couldn't afford to be anything but on the ball when her shift began again.

A cup of tea and twenty minutes with her shoes kicked off beneath a table would be bliss.

She was calculating if she had enough cash for food too when a dark figure loomed before her. Automatically she stepped to one side. So did he. Lucy stepped the other way to find he'd made the same manoeuvre.

That was when she took in the glossy, beautifully tooled shoes blocking her path.

Her nape prickled as she raised her gaze over an exquisitely tailored suit and cashmere overcoat. She gasped and sucked in a spicy scent she'd never forget if she lived to be a hundred.

'Domenico!'

Gun-metal grey eyes met hers from under straight black brows. The shock of him in the flesh rocked her back on her heels. She'd imagined him often, dreamt about him every night, but had forgotten how incredibly magnetic that deep gaze was.

Hungrily she took in those high cheekbones, the strong nose and hard jaw, the sensuous mouth. So familiar, so dear. Her heart bumped then catapulted into a gallop. She buried her hands deep in her pockets lest she reach for him as she did in her dreams.

He looked utterly gorgeous, but there were lines of strain around his eyes and the groove in his cheek scored deeper than before. He'd been working too hard.

'Lucy.' Just two syllables and her nerves danced a shimmy of delight. No one said her name as he did. No one made it sound half so appealing.

'What are you doing in London?'

'I have an important meeting.'

Of course he did. Domenico's world was full of important meetings. She'd followed his progress in the press these last couple of months, from the USA to Germany, China and back to Rome. Nothing had stopped his spectacular business success. Certainly not regret over her.

Still she couldn't bring herself to move. She stood, drinking him in, like a shaft of Italian sunshine on this grey English day.

'With you.'

'Sorry?' She'd lost the thread of the conversation.

'It's you I'm here to see.'

She shook her head. Of course she wanted to see him, but self-preservation cautioned it could only lead to catastrophe. She didn't have the willpower to say goodbye again. Getting over Domenico Volpe was even harder than she'd feared.

'It's true.'

'How did you find me?'

His eyebrows rose and she thought of the vast resources he'd used to find the truth about her past. He'd probably just clicked his fingers and hey presto!

'Why track me down?' What could he want after all this time?

Then it struck her. Domenico put family above

all. He was big on duty and making things right. Why else would he come?

She made herself meet his eyes, not letting him see her disappointment. 'You don't have to worry. You didn't get me pregnant.'

Domenico stared into her brilliant blue gaze and felt a knife slash of pain. The chances had been slim but still he'd hoped.

He made himself nod as if her news hadn't all but gutted him. 'Thank you for telling me.'

Crazy to have hoped so hard. He should have known nothing about this would be easy.

Looking into her wary face, having her so close, was more difficult than he'd imagined. She looked the same, more beautiful if possible, but the warmth was gone from her gaze and there was no sign of that rare wondrous smile he'd come to believe she saved for him. No sign of the cheeky, confident woman who'd brought him to his knees with her sexy flirting. Lucy held herself back as if expecting more pain.

Something plunged deep in his belly. Guilt sharpened its claws on his vitals.

'So there's no reason for us to meet.' She gave him a cool smile but he saw beyond it to her bewilderment. Either her mask of unconcern wasn't as good as it used to be or he was getting better at reading her.

Yet it was far too early to feel anything like hope.

'But we have things to discuss.' He reached for her elbow. 'Come. My hotel is just around the corner. We can talk there.'

He breathed in her honey and sunshine scent and pleasure slammed into him. His fingers tightened on her arm as he drew her along.

'I don't want to talk in your hotel suite.'

He should have known she'd resist. When had she made things easy? Nervous tension battled pleasure at her familiar obstinacy.

'Fine. We'll use the public rooms.' He managed a smile, despite the nerves tightening his belly. Surely if she didn't trust the privacy of his suite it was because he could still tempt her? The notion charged his hopes.

He eased his grip and he tucked her arm in his. She didn't resist and anticipation rose as he led her around a corner towards a familiar brick building decorated with flags.

'Signor Volpe. Madame.' The top-hatted doorman welcomed them and they stepped inside.

Instantly Domenico felt Lucy stiffen. He liked the quiet and the excellent service here but he took for granted its hushed opulence.

'We can go to my rooms if you'd prefer.' His lips brushed her hair as he leaned close. The scent of her drove his careful plans into a tangle of lust and nerves. He prayed she'd say yes.

'No. This is fine.' He felt her stand taller, taking in the elegance of the area before them. It reminded him of her spunk when faced with the glitterati at the opera in Rome. Lucy had stiffened her spine, kept her head up and won the admiration of many.

Minutes later they were seated in a secluded corner of the vast reception room. The décor was opulent—huge arched mirrors, enormous pillars with gilded capitals and the scent of hundreds of roses from the massed arrangements. Yet here at their small table, seated comfortably in the glow of a nearby lamp, they had an illusion of privacy.

Lucy avoided his gaze, rubbing at a stain on her black skirt.

Domenico dragged his eyes from the short skirt that revealed her stunning legs. He had to focus.

Panic stirred and he forced it down. This was the most important negotiation of his life and he couldn't let nerves wreck his chances.

'Your stepmother contacted me.'

Lucy jerked her head up. 'Why you?'

He shrugged. 'She'd read about me collecting you

from prison, and you being with me in Rome. It was the only place she could think of to reach you.'

Wariness was writ large on Lucy's face. 'What did she want? Money?'

'No.' He paused, remembering that difficult conversation. 'She wanted to talk with you.'

Lucy shook her head. 'I can't imagine why.'

'Apparently she wants to apologise.'

'And you believed her?' Lucy's face was taut with outrage but with something else too. Something that might have been hope.

Domenico's heart lightened. Lucy tried so hard to be tough and cold, yet always she responded with a good heart. Look at the way she'd taken to Chiara and the way she'd let him into her life. She'd given Pia a second chance. Maybe she'd do it again.

'I believe she was genuinely sorry for that article. She said she needed the money and thought she could handle the media. According to her, the reporter twisted most of what she said and conveniently removed any positive comments.'

He paused, waiting for her to consider.

'She said she didn't want to talk with you before because she felt so ashamed of what she'd done.'

Lucy gnawed her lip and he wanted to reach out and stop her. But he didn't have the right. She'd walked away from him and who could blame her?

Even now he couldn't believe he'd let her go. Twice now he'd missed his chance with Lucy. Finally he'd learnt his lesson!

'I'll think about calling her.'

'Good.' He nodded and sat back as a waiter appeared with their afternoon tea. He was glad for a distraction despite the urgency coiling his belly tight. For the first time he could remember he was *scared*, not able to predict the outcome of this meeting.

'So, is that all?' Her tone was brisk, yet she cradled her celadon-green cup as if needing warmth. He didn't even bother taking his tea. He wouldn't be able to hold it steady. Too much rode on this and he'd lost the facility to pretend it wasn't important.

'No. There's more.'

Her brows arched. 'What? Is there something wrong with the case against Bruno?' For the first time she looked truly shaken.

'Nothing like that. It's all going smoothly.'

Her relief was palpable, yet it struck him that she hadn't looked directly at him. Not since that moment on the street when he'd read shock and something he couldn't name in her eyes.

'And so?'

'And so.' He swallowed and leaned forward. 'I want to talk about us.'

'There is no *us*, Domenico.' Her expression was cool. Yet the way she said his name in that scratchy voice gave him hope. He might be fooling himself but he'd take all the encouragement he could get.

She put her cup down and he snatched her hand up. It trembled.

'Liar,' he whispered. 'There's always been an us. Even when I didn't trust myself to believe what I felt for you in the beginning. I felt the world crumble around me because I wanted you so much it hurt. I wanted you so much I cursed my brother for having you first. Can you believe it?'

'Domenico!' Her voice was a hoarse gasp. 'You can't be serious. Back then you hated me.'

'I thought I hated you because of the bolt of emotion I felt whenever I looked at you. It shook me to the core and it wasn't just lust. It was a…link I couldn't explain. A link I pretended didn't exist because I let myself be swayed by lies and my own jealous pride.' He heaved in a tight breath.

'You felt it too, didn't you, Lucy?'

Her eyes were huge in her pale face. With her blonde hair long enough now to brush her shoulders, she looked more like the innocent who'd stood in the dock all those years ago and stolen his soul.

She shook her head. 'No. I knew you hated me and I felt…'

'What? What did you feel, Lucy?' Urgency made him grip her hand harder.

'I can't explain it.' She looked away. 'A link, I suppose, from the start. But it wasn't right. It was just lust.'

Was that what she thought? He grimaced, knowing it was his fault she believed it.

'No, *carissima*, it wasn't just lust.'

She tugged her hand. 'Please, let me go.'

'Not until you look at me, Lucy.'

Reluctantly she turned her head and he felt again that blast of heat surging through his veins as their gazes melded. Domenico lifted her hand and kissed it. He turned it over and pressed his mouth to her palm and felt her shiver delicately.

With a sigh he released her hand and watched her cradle it in her lap as if it burned her. Just as his lips tingled where he'd caressed her sweet flesh.

'I was a fool to let you leave, Lucy. I've regretted it from the moment you went.'

'It wasn't a matter of you *letting* me go. It was my decision.'

'Only because I couldn't see what was before my eyes.'

'What are you saying, Domenico?'

'I'm saying what's between us is more important than lust. It always was, though I was too shallow to trust my instincts. I'm saying I want you with me, Lucy. In Rome, or here in Britain if you prefer. I want you in my life.'

There. He'd said it. He'd never asked that of any woman.

'I don't believe you.'

She looked like a queen surveying a troublesome subject. So proud. So feisty. So hurt. Seeing the pain etched around her pursed lips, shame rose.

'I was a fool to let you walk away but I was too proud to plead with you to stay.'

'I can't imagine you pleading for anything.'

'Can't you?' His lips twisted bitterly.

'No. You're too arrogant. Too sure of yourself.'

'Remind me never to come to you for a character reference. You know me too well.'

'What is it you want, Domenico? Is this some sort of game?'

'I was never more serious in my life.'

'Domenico?' Her eyes rounded as he slipped from his chair and knelt before hers. 'What are you doing?'

'Pleading, *carissima*.' And the hell of it was he didn't give a damn who saw him. All he cared about was convincing Lucy.

'I don't understand.' She blinked, her eyes over-bright and he reached to take her hand.

'Nor did I, in Rome. I was too full of myself. Too pleased with my success in setting things right, and too full of relief that finally I was doing right by you after all those wrongs. I didn't question what was happening between us.'

For the first time since he'd known her Lucy looked lost for words.

'I thought I had it all—the satisfaction of seeing justice done, and you in my bed, in my life.' He paused, the words harder now. 'I thought that was all I wanted, to enjoy the moment, to have your company and the phenomenal sex, as long as it lasted.'

Her hand clenched in his. 'I hadn't thought past that. When you called me on it I wasn't ready to face what I really wanted. Because what I wanted scared me.'

'Liar.' The whispered word shivered through him. 'You're never scared.'

Again he lifted her hand to his mouth, inhaling her warm scent, absorbing her taste. He couldn't bear the thought of not being allowed to touch her again.

'I was absolutely petrified. So petrified I couldn't think straight. It wasn't one of my finer moments. But when you reminded me you hadn't really been free from the moment you got out of jail, how could

I stop you? You deserved the right to the life you wanted.'

He searched her face but couldn't read her thoughts. Fear coursed through his bloodstream and his breathing came in short, hard stabs.

'Cut to the chase, Domenico. What *is* it you want? Do you want me as your lover while you're in England? Or in Rome—' she paused as if searching for words '—till you've had enough?'

'No! I want more. I want everything. I fell for you years ago on one magic day in Rome. Then later you were so beautiful and so stoic in the face of all that horror, I couldn't get you out of my mind.'

His heart pounded as he pressed her palm to his chest. Her touch gave him courage to go on.

'When we met again I fell for you all over again.'

She shook her head. 'You're talking about sex.'

'That too.' He smiled at her prim expression, remembering her in his bed. 'But actually I fell for the woman who made me feel like a new man.'

He sliced his free hand through the air. 'I can't explain, but with your honesty, your generosity and your pleasure in everything around you, I became different too. A man who didn't calculate every last item, who remembered what it was to enjoy life and to *feel*. I learned there's more to life than balance sheets and takeovers. There's caring and forgiveness.'

His words echoed into silence. His pulse drummed a staccato tattoo that surely convinced her as nothing else could, that he was genuine.

'I want to be with you. I want to live my life with you, wherever you are. I want to make a family with you and be with you always. I love you, Lucy.'

Finally the words ran out. He'd bared himself utterly. In his former life where control meant everything, that would have been unthinkable.

'Lucy? Say something.' His voice was hoarse.

'I say you're very long-winded, Signor Volpe. But I wouldn't have missed a moment of it.' She leaned forward and there were stars in her eyes. 'You could talk the birds from the trees if you wanted.'

Hope spilled as he saw her glorious smile. 'You're the only one I'm interested in. Will you have me, *tesoro*? Will you be mine?'

'Domenico—' she murmured his name as if savouring each syllable and every muscle cinched tight '—I've been yours for so long I can barely remember what it was like before you burst into my life.' She sighed and whispered in his ear, 'I love you, Domenico.'

'Carissima!'

Finally he was free to do what he'd longed to from

the moment he'd seen her in the street. He scooped her into his arms and kissed her so thoroughly he almost forgot to breathe. Breathing was overrated. With Lucy in his arms, who needed oxygen?

Eventually something, a faint noise, caught his attention. He lifted his head, smiling at the beatific glow on his beloved's face, and turned.

'Champagne, sir?' The waiter held a vintage bottle of his favourite bubbly.

'Excellent idea. In my suite. Now.'

The waiter nodded and melted discreetly away.

'Lucy?'

'Mmm?' She snuggled into his arms as he lifted her. 'How do you feel about having our honeymoon right here?'

Eyes the pure blue of an Italian summer sky met his and a pulse of emotion beat through him. 'I think first you need to persuade me to marry you.' Her smile was that of a temptress.

Domenico turned and carried her out of the room, oblivious to the stares and smiles of the other patrons. The world had never been so right.

'Ah,' he whispered in her ear. 'You know how I like rising to a challenge.'

* * * * *

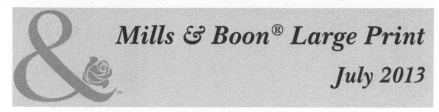

Mills & Boon® Large Print
July 2013

PLAYING THE DUTIFUL WIFE
Carol Marinelli

THE FALLEN GREEK BRIDE
Jane Porter

A SCANDAL, A SECRET, A BABY
Sharon Kendrick

THE NOTORIOUS GABRIEL DIAZ
Cathy Williams

A REPUTATION FOR REVENGE
Jennie Lucas

CAPTIVE IN THE SPOTLIGHT
Annie West

TAMING THE LAST ACOSTA
Susan Stephens

GUARDIAN TO THE HEIRESS
Margaret Way

LITTLE COWGIRL ON HIS DOORSTEP
Donna Alward

MISSION: SOLDIER TO DADDY
Soraya Lane

WINNING BACK HIS WIFE
Melissa McClone

Mills & Boon® Large Print
August 2013

MASTER OF HER VIRTUE
Miranda Lee

THE COST OF HER INNOCENCE
Jacqueline Baird

A TASTE OF THE FORBIDDEN
Carole Mortimer

COUNT VALIERI'S PRISONER
Sara Craven

THE MERCILESS TRAVIS WILDE
Sandra Marton

A GAME WITH ONE WINNER
Lynn Raye Harris

HEIR TO A DESERT LEGACY
Maisey Yates

SPARKS FLY WITH THE BILLIONAIRE
Marion Lennox

A DADDY FOR HER SONS
Raye Morgan

ALONG CAME TWINS...
Rebecca Winters

AN ACCIDENTAL FAMILY
Ami Weaver

0713 Rom LP